after eig

after eight- an aubrey stanton novel / avery stark

after eight

an Aubrey Stanton Crime

Novel

Book One

By Avery Stark

after eight- an aubrey stanton novel / avery stark

This book is dedicated to

the men and women

of law enforcement.

Copyright © 2019 by Avery Stark

All rights reserved. This book or any portion thereof may not be reproduced or used in any manner whatsoever without the express written permission of the publisher
except for the use of brief quotations in a book review.

To the extent that the image or images on the cover of this book depict a person or persons, such person or persons are merely models and are not intended to portray any character or characters featured in the book.

This is a work of fiction. Names, characters, businesses, places, events, locales, and incidents are either the products of the author's imagination or used in a fictitious manner. Any resemblance to actual persons, living or dead, or actual events is purely coincidental.

Cover design copyright: <u>Evgeny Atamanenko</u>
Printed in the United States of America

First Printing, 2019

Contents

Chapter 1

Chapter 2

Chapter 3

Chapter 4

Chapter 5

Chapter 6

Chapter 7

Chapter 8

Chapter 9

Chapter 10

Chapter 11

Chapter 12

Chapter 13

Chapter 14

Chapter 15

Chapter 16

Chapter 17

Chapter 18

Chapter 19

Chapter 20

Chapter 21

Chapter 22

Chapter 23

Chapter 24

Acknowledgments

Solace Preview-Aubrey Stanton Book 2

> "It's no use going back to yesterday
> because I was a different person then."
> -Lewis Carroll, Alice's Adventures in Wonderland

Prologue

Spencer, Michigan 1963

Everyone has a defining moment in their lives, not many people have two at merely eight years old. Aubrey Stanton was an exception. The first occurred in the winter of 1962 when her brother, Tom, abandoned her in the small woods near their home, so he could join his friends at the small fire they'd made.

"Tom, I want to go home. I'm cold," Aubrey complained, teeth chattering.

"Don't be such a baby. If you want to go, go. I'm having fun with John and Ricky," Tom grumbled, not for the first time that day.

Nearly frostbitten, she trudged through the tall grass, slipping and falling on icy spots until she reached the busy street. Aubrey watched the traffic whizz by her and gauged the time between cars. When she saw a break, she made a mad dash to the other side and found her way home.

Jayne Stanton, her mother, face red with anger, dragged her into the car to look for her brother.

"What on earth is wrong with you, Aubrey?" she scolded. "Why didn't you stay with Tom?"

"He wanted to play with his friends, and I was cold." Her voice trembled under her mother's wrath.

It occurred to Aubrey how her mom's concern focused on finding her brother, and her anger seemed directed at her for leaving him, rather than taking care of Aubrey's blue, freezing fingers and feet.

Having braved the busy highway and her mother's wrath at having left behind an older brother in the field, Aubrey knew she had to be responsible for herself instead of relying on others to take care of her. From this point on, she would make her own decisions about where she went and who she wanted to be.

Aubrey would always fight for the underdog. She would learn to protect herself and others, caring for those who could not care for themselves. She vowed she would never allow someone else to choose her fate. Aubrey wasn't sure how she would achieve these things but felt the strength of her conviction would guide her.

Her first defining moment would shape her character.

****

The second moment was the following fall when President John F. Kennedy was assassinated in Dallas, Texas on November 22, 1963. After being dismissed early from school, Aubrey ran home and changed into her Brownie uniform for the weekly meeting at Mrs. Jackson's house. She looked forward to the meeting with all her friends every week. Mrs. Jackson laughed and gave each girl a hug when they arrived, always had snacks and games to play. But that day, when she arrived, her scout leader told her to go back home. Since the president had been killed, there would not be a meeting that day.

Angry at her mother for not telling her the meeting was canceled, Aubrey changed her clothes and took her little terrier-mix puppy, Kizzy, to the park. Some undeveloped areas, covered in a variety of trees and bushes, were Aubrey's favorite spots to take her puppy. She pretended to be an explorer, and the dog ran loose to chase squirrels and sniff odd odors. She carried a long stick to fend off any imaginary, ferocious beasts.

"Take that, you evil bear," she shouted and stabbed at a large bush.

Kizzy was jumping around in the fallen leaves, then suddenly stopped. Nose to the ground, she ran behind a fallen tree trunk and started barking.

"What did you find, girl?"

Aubrey ran to see what Kizzy had found, and there, in the dead and discolored leaves, was a pale hand, missing chunks of flesh. *That looks like a hand. Why is it so white?* She looked closer.

Having never seen a dead body, Aubrey was both repulsed and curious. She used her stick to prod the body. Pushing away several bits of debris, a pallid and dirty face appeared, semi-hidden in the half-decomposed vegetation.

At first, she didn't recognize the face of her best friend, who'd been absent from school all week. Everyone believed she had the flu, as Tom had the week before. Realization struck.

"Oh! It's Lori." Aubrey, eyes wide, spun around, looking for anyone else, older and wiser to tell, but she was alone in the park. She gagged and struggled not to vomit.

She yelled to Kizzy, who had wandered away, "Come on, girl. We gotta get outta here and go home. I hafta tell Mom."

Sobbing at her discovery, Aubrey raced home to tell her mother about Lori, with Kizzy close on her heels. She found her mother resting in her bedroom when she arrived.

The family rule didn't allow children in her parent's bedroom. Aubrey stood at the doorway, shaking and trying to stop her voice from quivering. "M...Mom, Kizzy f...found …."

With a cloth covering her eyes, her mother didn't bother looking at her daughter and said, "Aubrey, Mommy's not feeling very well right now. Can you go and play in your room, please?"

"But, Mom…"

"No buts, Aubrey. Go play. I'm exhausted and need a nap."

Aubrey knew all too well when she heard her mother's stern voice, she'd be unwilling to hear more. She turned away, head lowered. Frustrated over her mother's dismissal, she dashed across the hall to her bedroom, closed her door, flung herself on the bed, and cried into Kizzy's soft fur. Kizzy, always her loyal friend, lay next to Aubrey, licking her tears away.

"What am I going to do, Kizzy? Should I tell Tom?" she asked as she wiped her eyes.

The dog cocked her head as if thinking about the problem.

"Yes, you're right. Tom'll know what to do next. He's probably in the basement working on one of his experiments again. I hope it's not as smelly as the last one, or as smoky as the one before that."

On an unusually frigid day a week before, Tom had found a frozen squirrel in the backyard. He left it on top of the furnace to thaw out, intending to dissect it once it was thoroughly soft. He never got the chance. As it warmed up, the entire house reeked of a dead animal. Their parents scolded him, telling him not to do it again. They didn't punish him. He was forever doing what Aubrey thought were crazy things.

Aubrey and Kizzy went to the basement to tell Tom. He could always be found there, playing with his chemistry set in the tiny room beneath the stairs.

"Hey, Tom? I need your help."

"Yeah, Squirt, what do you want? I'm busy."

"Well, Kizzy and I found something in the park. I'm not sure what to do. Mom wouldn't let me tell her. She said she didn't feel well and needed a nap. Her angry voice told me to go play."

"So? What did you find? A treasure chest? Was it too heavy to carry home? Another lost baseball mitt? What?" Tom laughed, turning back to his experiment. A beaker bubbled with blue liquid inside over a tiny flame.

"We found my friend, Lori. In the leaves." She sniffled. "She's ... dead. Her face was all white. It looked like animals had eaten part of her arm and hand." Aubrey gagged as she remembered the scene, ghost-like traces of tears trailed down her cheeks.

She had Tom's attention. "Really? Are you jokin' around? It's not funny, ya know," he chastised, frowning at his little sister.

"No, really. She was lying on the ground. She looked cold. I got scared, and Kizzy and I ran home." Her lip trembled as she fought not to cry again.

"You said Mom's sleeping?" He lifted his eyebrows.

"Yeah, I think she has one of her headaches. She was really upset earlier when I came home from school ... ya know, cuz President Kennedy got killed. It's starting to get dark. I don't like to think of Lori out there all night."

Aubrey shuffled her feet. "I think you should wake up Mom. She won't get as mad at you for interrupting her nap. Dad won't be home for a while."

"Was there a lot of blood? Was her head bashed in, or anything?" Tom asked, eyes wide, excitement evident in his voice.

"Yuck, no. I didn't see anything like that. As soon as I saw who it was, I got scared and ran home."

"Too bad. Yeah, we need to tell Mom. She'll call the police." Tom turned off his Bunsen burner.

The children hurried upstairs to their mother's room. Standing in the bedroom doorway, Tom shouted, "Mom, wake up. We have something to tell you."

"Tom, Aubrey," their mother spit out their names. "Didn't I tell you I wasn't feeling well? Why are you shouting?" She removed her sleeping mask. "What's going on?"

"Aubrey found a dead girl in the park. I knew we should tell you right away 'cuz it's gettin' dark outside, and the police might have trouble finding her."

"What? A dead girl? Aubrey, are you sure? Why didn't you tell me earlier?" Jayne sat up and, caught in the covers, stumbled out of the bed.

"I tried to tell you before. You told me to go to my room. I saw my friend, Lori, on the ground. She was all white, and I think animals had eaten part of her. It was awful, so Kizzy and I came home to tell you."

"Okay, okay, give me a few minutes. I need to fix my face and hair." She waved her hand at the children as if brushing away irritating flies.

"Mom, shouldn't you call the cops right away?" Tom asked.

"If she's dead, she's not going anywhere," Jayne said, narrowing her eyes. "Give me a minute. I'll call the police when I'm presentable. You two go wait in your rooms." She coughed, her raspy voice was thick with nicotine residue. "This is certainly not helping my headache. I need a cigarette. What a day." She reached for her pack of Pall Malls, lighting one as she walked to the bathroom.

Thirty minutes later, Aubrey heard her mother call the police to make the report. She was surprised by the lack of concern in her mother's voice as she explained to the person on the other end of the phone what she was calling about.

Jayne hung up the phone and opened Aubrey's bedroom door. "They'll be here soon. I'm sure the police will want to talk to you. Change your clothes, they're dirty. And don't forget to call him, 'sir.' You know how your father feels about showing respect to adults."

"Yes, ma'am," Aubrey replied.

Twenty minutes later, the police arrived, asking to speak with Aubrey.

She was surprised when only one man, dressed in a suit, instead of a uniform, stood in the living room. She expected several officers, all in their neat uniforms and badges, to appear. Instead, the man knelt in front of her. She liked his nice eyes, and when he spoke, his voice was gentle.

"Hi, honey, I'm Detective Rollins. I understand you found something in the park today?"

"Well, Kizzy actually found her," Aubrey said, eyes lowered, lip quivering.

"Kizzy?" He raised his eyebrows in question.

"Kizzy's my dog." Aubrey pointed to the dog sitting in the kitchen, then blurted, "She found Lori covered in leaves behind a tree trunk. She was lying there, all white … and … kinda chewed up a little. Lori's my best friend … or was …," her mother nudged her, "sir." She stumbled over the words, as she realized she'd forgotten to say 'sir' to the man like her father always demanded.

"It's okay, you're doing fine. I know this is hard." Rollins looked at her with kind eyes. "When you say chewed up? You mean by animals?"

"Yes, sir. That's what it looked like."

"Aubrey, do you think you could find this place again?"

"Yes, sir. But can't I tell you where she is? Do I really have to look at her again? She looked awful. I was scared to stay there." Aubrey bit the inside of her lower lip to keep her tears from falling. She wanted to be tough like Tom, who stood next to her, with wide-eyed fascination.

"Detective Rollins, please," her mom pleaded, in the phony-concerned voice she used for teachers and doctors, and apparently, policemen. "Aubrey is only eight years old. Isn't there another way to do this? This girl, Lo…Lo...Lorraine was her friend, after all. Can't she tell you where it is?"

Aubrey looked at her mother, puzzled. *Mom knows her name is Lori, why did she say Lorraine? My friend is not an 'it' either.* She frowned, trying to understand her mother's response.

"Mrs. Stanton, I understand how difficult this must be for your daughter, but since it'll be dark soon, it'll be hard to find *Lori* by ourselves. If Aubrey can show us where *she* is, it will be easier."

I like this detective. I know he'll take care of Lori. Aubrey smiled.

He took a deep breath, let it out, and continued in a more conciliatory tone, "Look, I'm sure you want us to notify her parents as soon as possible and start searching for whoever did this, right?"

He turned to Aubrey. "No, you won't have to look at her again. I'll make sure of it. You'll just have to point out where she is."

"Well, yes, of course, we want to help." Her mother glared at Rollins and placed her hand on Aubrey's shoulder. "Do you think you can do this for the detective? I'll be there with you the whole time. Tom, you stay here and wait for your dad."

Tom pouted. "Aw, Mom. I want to go, too."

"No, stop whining. You stay here. There's no reason for you to go, and your dad will need to know where we went if he gets home before us. Aubrey, can you do this?"

"Sure, Mom. I can find her again. If I bring Kizzy, it'll be even faster." *Maybe Mom'll be proud of me, for once, if I help the detective.*

Detective Rollins, Mrs. Stanton, Aubrey, and Kizzy climbed into his unmarked car. Aubrey had hoped for sirens and lights, but it looked like any other car to her. They drove to the park and pulled up on Garrison Street, next to the area where Aubrey indicated she'd been playing. Three other police officers arrived to help. Dusk was falling, so they turned on their flashlights to begin the search. Kizzy had no trouble finding the body again. Aubrey turned her head away, unable to look at her friend.

"Officer Mills, can you place the crime scene tape all around this area, please?" Detective Rollins asked.

"I'll get right on it, Detective."

She watched as Officer Mills placed the yellow tape around the immediate vicinity. The organized chaos that followed mesmerized her. The coroner arrived to examine the body, and crime scene techs swarmed the area looking for evidence. Police officers set up bright lights around the trees, as darkness rolled in.

"Thanks so much for your help, Aubrey." Rollins petted the dog. "We might not have found her as easily without Kizzy. I'm so sorry this happened to you. We'll take good care of Lori from here." The detective turned to Mrs. Stanton. "I'm sorry this took so long. I'll have a patrolman take you home in a minute."

Rollins gestured to a nearby officer, "Please take Aubrey and Kizzy back to my car and get them settled. I need to talk to her mother for a minute."

He looked at Mrs. Stanton, who was fidgeting nearby. "Thank you for letting your daughter help us. She's a brave girl. You should be proud of her." His caring words fell on deaf ears. "We've been quietly looking for Lori when she didn't come home after school on Monday. We thought she might have run away since she'd done it before. We didn't want to alarm everyone if that was the case. This is not the ending we'd hoped for."

"Well, of course not. I'd like to go home now. It's been a trying day." She lit her cigarette.

"Right away, ma'am, but you can't smoke in my car." Rollins shook his head. He had one of the police officers drive them to the house.

****

When Aubrey's father arrived home, Jayne told him, "It was a horrible day. Aubrey found a dead girl in the park. I had to call the police, and we had to go back to the park to find her. Aubrey is upset, of course. I have a headache, the president is dead. What's next?"

She threw together a dinner of leftover spaghetti, salad, and garlic bread, and they sat at their respective places at the dining room table.

Tom had loads of questions, but his father's unyielding voice silenced him. "I think we've all had enough excitement today, with President Kennedy assassinated, and now this poor girl is dead, too. Let's talk about something else."

No one had anything more to say, and both children knew better than to defy their father. They ate the rest of their dinner in silence, with eyes downcast on their plates.

Tom and Aubrey went to bed while their parents talked late into the night about things Aubrey couldn't hear. She thought about all the fun things she and Lori had done together and what a great friend she'd been. She loved going to Lori's house because Mrs. Harris always had cookies for the girls. Lori's mom was so nice, always asking about Aubrey's day, something her own mother rarely did. She tossed and turned, seeing poor, dead Lori's face every time she closed her eyes. She cuddled closer to Kizzy, and shortly before dawn, fell asleep.

Detective Rollins, with his compassion and thoughtfulness, impressed Aubrey. She recognized the importance of his job and helping people. She decided to become a police officer. Aubrey wanted to help solve crimes like Lori's murder. She made a promise to herself to do everything she could to become one.

This second defining moment would shape her career.

Chapter 1

Thirteen years later, in June 1976, newly graduated Police Officer Aubrey Stanton's face beamed with joy as she recited her oath to protect the people of Spencer, Michigan.

" I, Aubrey Stanton, do solemnly swear that I will support and defend the Constitution of the United States and the Constitution of the State of Michigan against all enemies, foreign and domestic; that I will bear true faith and allegiance; that I take this obligation freely, without any mental reservation or purpose of evasion; and that I will well and faithfully discharge the duties upon which I am about to enter."

She was the only woman graduating from this class. Two others had dropped out after the first week. Like them, Aubrey had been ridiculed, harassed, hazed and bullied, but she was determined to make it through the six-month course. Perhaps she had more motivation than the other candidates.

The Spencer Police had searched for two long years to find Lori Harris's killer. The coroner officially confirmed

Aubrey's friend had been murdered in one place and dumped in the park. Unfortunately, he found no clues on the body or surrounding areas to help with the investigation. Detective Rollins visited Aubrey multiple times to ask questions over and over again, but Aubrey had no new answers, and the police had no new leads, so they'd let it become cold. It was still an open, unsolved case but no longer active. She missed his visits and encouragement.

The night she and her dog, Kizzy, discovered Lori, Aubrey decided to become a police officer, but once the cops ran out of leads to catch Lori's killer, Aubrey resolved to become a detective someday. She vowed to find and arrest whoever was responsible for her death and bring the murderer to justice. Aubrey felt Lori deserved peace, and she frequently wondered what sort of adult she would have become if her path hadn't crossed a killer's. Graduating from the academy was the first step in fulfilling her promise to her friend.

None of Aubrey's family had come to watch her walk across the stage to receive her Basic Police Officer Certificate and shake hands with the city officials. She was grateful for the handful of friends, including her life-long friend, Donna, who'd arrived to celebrate Aubrey's new career.

"Hey, Aubrey," Donna shouted above the din of cheering. "Where's your mom and dad?"

"Oh, you know, Donna, they're too busy hunting for new partners, and Tom's working at a new job in a tiny town in California. Did you know he's recently been elected County Coroner as well, although I can't understand how. As far as I know, Tom doesn't have any training in forensics or anatomy."

I have to remember to ask him about it. He might be helpful in my future investigations.

"That's Tom for you, always doing something unexpected. That's okay, my friend. We're here." She indicated the small group of other friends who'd shown up to help celebrate the beginning of Aubrey's new career.

"Thank you all for coming. Let's go party."

The group left the ceremony amid hugs, handshakes, and back slaps on the new officers. She didn't see Detective Rollins standing in the background, smiling.

****

Aubrey had made a few male friends from the academy after they realized she wasn't going anywhere, despite their efforts. A couple of the guys had admitted they admired her persistence. Unfortunately, they would be working in other cities.

Except for Scott Fuller. He was adamant about not working with a female cop. Aubrey hoped she wouldn't ever be partnered with this jerk or need him as her back-up. Scott, at twenty-five, was the epitome of the all-American high school jock. Attractive on the outside: six-foot-tall, blue eyes, thick, dirty blond hair, and powerfully built, he was equally as ugly on the inside: petty, jealous, cruel, and vindictive, but *always* charming to the instructors. It made for a wicked combination.

She had been continuously on guard with him. Friendly one moment, and the next, he'd shove, elbow, even ram her into walls, whenever she was near. He was discreet … the instructors never saw anything. She hated him.

Aubrey didn't date in high school. The boys seemed intimidated by her. Her self-confidence made her an outcast among the boys, and since she wasn't obsessed with her hair or make-up, it also separated her from most of the girls. She thought things might be different with older, more mature boys at the community college where she'd earned her Associate's Degree in Criminal Justice. Once again, she was disappointed but shrugged it off. She didn't need or want a boyfriend who couldn't handle her independence, intelligence, and strong will. Her time would come. At twenty-one years old, she had plenty of time for romance.

Monday would be her first day on the job, and she knew she would have a Field Training Officer, or FTO, assigned. The academy taught her laws and rules, how to subdue a person resisting arrest, and defend herself, but her FTO would give her experience in the real world, and her intuition would guide her.

* * * *

Monday morning came bright and early for Aubrey. She'd hardly slept the night before. In the past, Kizzy would have jumped up at the alarm, ready for action, but she wasn't as spry as she'd once been. She looked at Aubrey, closed her eyes, and went back to sleep. Aubrey got up, showered, and dressed in a navy blue T-shirt and jeans. The department would supply her uniforms. She was giddy with anticipation about finally wearing one every day.

She fixed juice and a bagel for breakfast and filled Kizzy's bowls with food and fresh water. When the dog woke up, she would use her doggy door to go outside into the backyard and do her business. Aubrey walked out of the small rental house where she'd lived for the past three years, to start the first day of her new life.

When she arrived at the police station, the corporal at the front desk directed her down the hallway to Sergeant Mills. The man exuded an air of authority in spite of his five-foot-six stature, heavy jowls, and pot-belly. His appearance and attitude reminded Aubrey of a weary, overweight bulldog, with his semi-bald, liver-spotted pate, large ears, and pronounced underbite.

He gave her two sets of uniforms, a pair of sturdy, black shoes, and a gun belt, including a baton, handcuffs, her service weapon, a nine millimeter Smith & Wesson semi-automatic handgun, and two boxes of ammunition.

"Get changed and return to the squad room for roll call. You have ten minutes. Get moving," the sergeant said as he pointed the way to the locker room.

Aubrey heard loud talking and laughing coming from the room he'd indicated and was curious since she was the only female officer in the department. When she opened the door, fusty, damp, distinctly male odors assaulted her. The room swarmed with men in various stages of undress. In unison, they glanced up at her, turned, and went back to their conversations. She shut the door, embarrassed at intruding. *Oh, my God. How did I not hear all those men's voices?* She sighed. *I wonder how long I'll be teased about that little blunder?*

She returned to the sergeant. "Excuse me, Sarge, where is the women's locker room?"

"There isn't one. Use the one we have, or use the public restroom to change in."

"Um ... ok. Thanks, Sergeant." *I wonder when they plan to create one?*

Aubrey found the tiny, filthy women's restroom. A festering stench permeated the space, stinging her nostrils. Cleaning it was apparently no one's priority. The wastebasket overflowed, feminine hygiene products stuck out from the top and stuck to the floor, and unidentifiable black grime coated the sink. Cigarette butts littered the tiles, along with wads of chewed gum. Aubrey was revolted but knew she had a limited amount of time to don her uniform and accessories. She had no choice. If this would be her 'locker' room, she'd bring cleaning supplies to take care of the mess the next morning.

Rushing to change and not wanting to be late for roll call on her first day, Aubrey hung one uniform in an empty stall and put the other one on. The huge shirt hung off her slender frame, and the pants were gigantic at the waist and four inches too long. She tucked in the shirttails as best she could and rolled up the pant legs and shirt sleeves, cinching her belt to its last notch. Even the tie made it seem she was playing dress-up in her father's closet. She put the shoes on and found them to be two sizes too large. She stuffed paper towels in the toes and tied them as tight as she could. She couldn't wear the too-small hat. At least her gun belt fit.

Aubrey looked in the cloudy, dirty, and rusted mirror. Her eyes were glassy with unshed tears and a lump formed in her throat. She knew she looked ridiculous. This was not how she'd envisioned her first day. *There's nothing to be proud about in this get-up.*

Aubrey spun around, fiercely swiped at her eyes, hung her jeans with her spare uniform, placed her tennis shoes on the grimy floor, and scribbled "Out of Order" on a paper towel, so no one would enter her 'closet.' Without other options, she used a relatively fresh wad of used gum to affix her sign to the door, washed her face and hands. Since it was a public restroom, she shoved her few personal things into her cavernous pants pockets.

Aubrey pulled herself up to her full five-foot-seven-and-a-half height and walked, with as much dignity as she could muster, to the squad room. As she entered, everyone started laughing. Scott Fuller's guffaws reverberated loudest. Determined not to turn tail and run, she clenched her jaw, kept her expression neutral, and took the only empty seat, directly in front of Fuller.

The sergeant walked in, scrutinized Aubrey, sighed, and said, "All right, all right, settle down, everyone. In case you haven't noticed ... which is hard not to ... we have two new officers starting today, Aubrey Stanton and Scott Fuller. I expect all of you to show them how we do things here, and mostly, remember how you felt your first day on the job."

Aubrey could feel the hostility emanating from Fuller, sitting behind her. Sergeant Mills glanced around the room and gave individual officers a lengthier glare than others, then continued, directing his comments to Aubrey and Scott. "Officer Stanton, FTO McLain will be your training officer for the next twelve weeks. Officer Fuller, yours is FTO Hopkins. Listen to them, do as they say, and don't do anything stupid. Now, everyone get going and be safe out there."

As the officers spilled out of the squad room, Fuller gave Aubrey a discreet shove into the wall and muttered, "What the hell are you doing here anyway?"

There was no time to respond as her FTO yelled, "Stanton, get out here."

* * * *

Her first day on patrol was nothing like Aubrey anticipated. She'd imagined catching crooks, settling disputes, or maybe helping a downtrodden person. Instead, they drove around, stopped for coffee, drove around again, stopped for lunch, and drove around some more. At one point, an elderly woman, with blue-tinted, carefully coiffed hair, wearing a bright pink cardigan and propping herself on a walker with tennis ball shoes, waved them down. *Now here's a lady who can use some help.* But the woman only wanted to tell them she appreciated their protection. Aubrey was disappointed. They headed back to the station.

FTO McLain had said as little as possible all day, except, as they pulled into the police parking lot, he told her, "Get shoes the right size and have your uniforms tailored because you look unprofessional. And get a hat that fits, for God's sake."

"This is what the sergeant gave me. It's not my fault they don't fit," Aubrey retorted.

"You must not have paid attention in the academy," said the FTO, sneering. "They always explain you need to have your uniform fitted and get shoes the right size before your first day. You should have stopped by and picked them up on Friday. Get it done today, or you can't go out with me tomorrow."

"Okay, I will," Aubrey replied with a clenched jaw. She knew they'd never mentioned this in the academy, and she had no idea how to go about it. Aubrey would figure it out, though. She'd always been good at figuring out difficult things.

They turned in their squad car and clocked out. Aubrey was disheartened but hoped tomorrow would be better. When she entered the restroom to change, she found her tennis shoes filled with shaving cream. She smiled, things were going to be fine.

Chapter 2

A year later, Aubrey was riding solo and loving her job. After patrolling her section of the city for a couple hours, her stomach rumbled. She drove to the nearest convenience store for a snack. The store sat in the middle of a small strip mall. She had to park a few stores down instead of in front, her usual spot. It was a beautiful day, and she enjoyed the short walk in the fresh air. Aubrey entered the store, nodded to the clerk, and walked down the farthest aisle from the door, to get a cold drink.

As she reached to grab a cherry-flavored cola, she heard the front door burst open. Aubrey cautiously walked up the aisle to get a better look.

"Hand over the money … *now.*" A twenty-something man yelled at the frightened clerk.

He must not realize I'm here.

The man held a gun to the clerk's head. Aubrey tossed a can of beans over the display shelves toward the store windows. Confused, the robber pointed his gun down the empty aisle.

"Who's there?" he demanded.

Aubrey moved closer, gun drawn.

The clerk took advantage of the distraction and ducked under the counter. Protected behind a drinks case, Aubrey drew her weapon and commanded, *"Police, drop your weapon. Do it now."*

The gunman turned toward Aubrey's voice and fired. The display of potato chips exploded near her face. Aubrey fired back, the man screamed and grabbed his arm, dropping his gun. The slug's impact spun him around. He lost his balance and fell. She sprinted up the aisle, grabbed his arm, and pushed him, face first, against the floor. She dug her knee into the small of his back, kicked the compact, cheap *Saturday Night Special* away from them, and handcuffed him.

Ignoring his wound, she yanked him to his feet, giving him the Miranda warning. "You have the right to remain silent —."

Aubrey placed the robber in the back of her squad car, picked up her radio mike, and said, "I need a road sergeant and a *bus* for a wounded suspect." She'd learned the shorthand for ambulance and other things quickly during her time with her FTO.

The road sergeant would handle the crime scene. She knew he would take her duty weapon and put her on administrative leave. The action was standard procedure in an officer-involved shooting. Crime scene investigators would show up to collect the evidence, including the bullet meant for her.

While she waited for the ambulance to arrive, her hands shook. It was the first time she'd shot anyone. *How silly of me. C'mon hands, knock it off. I did a good thing, my job.* She clasped her hands together to stop the tremors and leaned on the hood of her car. *I know it's policy to see a psychologist when you actually shoot a person, but I'm okay. I'm glad I didn't kill him. That might be different. I hope I never have to.*

Her road sergeant drove up a minute after the ambulance arrived. He took her gun, patted her on the shoulder, muttered, "Good job, Rookie," and walked away.

The EMTs took the would-be thief. She was done for the day after she wrote up a report on the incident. She would have the next couple days off as well.

The department had recently incorporated a requirement for a psychologist's fitness review after any trauma on the job. The report was becoming more common among police departments but wasn't widespread yet. She was scheduled for counseling over the next several weeks. *There's nothing like the adrenaline rush I felt from that incident. I love my job.*

* * * *

After a brief inquest, Aubrey was cleared of any wrongdoing. The morning she returned to duty, Aubrey arrived at the police station two hours early, ready to begin her search for Lori's killer. After the convenience store incident and the confidence Aubrey felt during the standoff, it was time to review Lori's case. She knew she didn't have the training the detectives had been given but wanted to start looking at the evidence in the case. Aubrey wanted to know all the facts and determine whether there were any loose ends to investigate. Although she felt self-assured in her role as a patrol officer, she understood how slim the odds of her finding Lori's killer were. *It'll give me some experience reviewing files and looking for unanswered questions, at least. I hope the sarge will agree.* She found Sergeant Mills at his desk.

"Good morning, Sergeant. I brought you coffee ... fresh from the pot. Black, right?"

"Good morning, Officer Stanton." His eyes narrowed, revealing his suspicion at the gesture. "I'll take the coffee. You've never brought me a cup before. So, what do you want?"

"You caught me. I do have a favor to ask. I'd like to work on a cold case, the Lori Harris file."

"Normally, a detective is assigned a cold case, and you're not one. You haven't had the training required. Why are you interested in it?" he asked with a knowing look.

"Well, it's been cold for a while, and you know I do *want* to become a detective. I thought I could follow up on some things … on my own time. You never know, I might stumble on something Detective Rollins missed." Her foot tapped a staccato beat on the tile floor.

Aubrey didn't want Mills to know Lori was her friend. She was afraid he'd say it was too close to home for her to be objective. She stood waiting and trying not to fidget while he pondered her request.

"I remember you were the one who found her body. You were how old? Seven … eight? I can understand why you want to solve it." Mills paused, chewed on his bottom lip as he considered her request.

Busted. I forgot he was at the scene that night. So much for me keeping it secret. I don't know if it's a good thing or not that he was there.

"It's more than that, sir. Lori was my best friend. I feel if I hadn't let her leave school alone that day, she would still be alive. In my head, I know it's not, but in my heart, I do."

Mills cocked his head, looking at her. "I'm glad you know it's not your fault. Things happen. But I think it's cold enough, you can't get into trouble. If you do it on your own time, *and* if you immediately report to me anything you find, I'll let you work it. I also want a weekly report on whatever you do with it."

"Thanks, Sarge. Do I need anything from you to request the binder?"

"I'll call down to the file room and let them know you're coming. This is against my better judgment. Don't screw up and don't let it get in the way of your regular duties." Mills scowled as he called the records room to tell the officer-in-charge she'd been assigned to the case. He shook his head and muttered, "I'm not sure this is a smart move. It may be a disaster waiting to happen."

Aubrey fast-walked down to the basement where the files and evidence were stored. She requested the blue binder, or what detectives called the murder book, which chronicled the case from the moment Lori's parents had reported her missing. It included the time Detective Rollins was dispatched to Aubrey's house in 1963, up to the point when it became a cold case, two years later.

Surprised at seeing a rookie cop asking for a blue binder, Sergeant Piper, the officer-in-charge of the file room, asked, "So, you've been on the force, what, a year, and you think you can solve a cold one?" he asked her. "Have you even been involved in a homicide investigation before?"

Aubrey smiled, shrugged, and replied, "In a way, yes. I want to study the case, it's personal for me."

"Well, good luck," Piper said, as he handed over the blue binder. "If you need the evidence box, let me know, and I'll get it for you ... but there's not much in it."

"Thanks." Aubrey signed out the file and returned to the squad room where it would be quiet, and she'd have space to spread things out.

Aubrey opened the binder. She didn't want the images distracting her from the facts, so she set aside the crime photos, and started with the initial police report. As she read through the basics, Aubrey remembered the day she and Kizzy discovered Lori, dead in the park, covered in leaves and partially eaten by animals. Scared and repulsed, she'd run home, crying. For the first time in years, she felt the revulsion and anger again at whoever had done it.

The report stated, *The victim appeared to have been sexually assaulted before being stabbed repeatedly in the abdomen, back, and chest. Based on lack of blood or other evidence, park location is the secondary site; it appears victim was assaulted in an unknown location.*

Aubrey hadn't known those details. Her parents had forbidden her to read newspaper articles, and refused to discuss the case in her presence. *I'm sure they were only trying to protect me. At eight years old, I know I couldn't have handled all this gruesome information.*

After Aubrey read the police report, she flipped to the autopsy findings.

Multiple incised and stab wounds are present on the chest, abdomen, and back. There are eighteen on the chest and back, twelve in the abdomen, and no defensive incised wounds on the right or left hands or forearms. Most of the sharp-force injuries present are incised wounds, and most of the stab wounds are penetrating of the body cavities, except as detailed below. There are also blunt-force injuries and overlying rib fractures as below.

Trace materials on tape from right shoulder/chest; possibly small glass fragment from left upper chest; trace materials on tape from left shoulder/neck/chest; trace materials on tape from chest; glass fragments from back; possible glass fragments from chest; hairs adherent to right and left sleeves of shirt; hairs adherent to left hand; one (1) hair from inside the mouth; right fingernail clippings; left fingernail clippings; and adherent hairs from right hand. Purple-and red-topped tubes of blood are also collected and sent to the lab.

Hair? Glass fragments? Aubrey wondered. *Wouldn't those have helped locate a suspect?* She searched for additional clues in the photos from the autopsy and crime scene. Aubrey had seen plenty of grisly pictures at the academy but never those of a close friend. Averting her gaze and taking deep breaths, she was able to settle her stomach. *C'mon now, I've seen worse at the academy.* She put her brain into *cop-mode* and looked again at the graphic photos.

Due to the amount of debris covering the body when she initially found the victim, Aubrey hadn't seen the stab wounds before. She was both mesmerized and appalled by the savagery. *How could anyone carry out such a horrific act against an eight-year-old girl? This small town doesn't usually have murders, much less the killing of children.*

Aubrey took notes from the photos, the autopsy report, and the detective's comments. *I should look up Detective Rollins and ask him a few questions. After all, he certainly asked me plenty of 'em. Maybe he can tell me things that aren't in this book.*

Against regulations, shielding her activity from anyone passing by, she made a copy of the book for herself, securing it in her car. When she returned the original binder to Sergeant Piper, she requested the evidence box and completed the form. Aubrey needed to look at what the techs had found at the scene.

"There's not much to see in the evidence box, but I'll get it for you. Why are you so interested in this case? Trying to be a detective so soon?" Piper smirked but studied her.

Makes no difference now who knows. "The victim was a friend of mine. I was always interested in the case and want to review what was found. Detective Rollins ran out of leads on the case. Would you happen to know where he lives now? I'd like to see him and ask some questions," she said, as he walked away from her, down the aisle looking for the correct box.

"Here it is. Sign this chain of custody form first. There's an inventory of the items in the box. Remember, each bag inside is recorded on this sheet, sealed, dated, and initialed by the officer who checked it in. Do not mess with any seals, do not open any bags, and make sure everything on this list is still in the box when you bring it back to me.

"Don't leave it lying around either. If you don't finish looking through it and have to leave, bring it back and check it out again when you're ready. You have to return it in exactly the same condition as you're taking it now. Got it?"

Aubrey nodded as he placed the signed document on the *Evidence Sign Out Sheet* clipboard on his desk.

Piper explained, "Detective Rollins retired from the department five years ago. *Personnel* would have his information. You can get the most recent address and phone number we have on file. Doesn't mean he's still there, but it's a starting point." He leaned back, furrowed his brow, and with arms crossed, scanned Aubrey's face. "Are you *sure* you want to do this? You might not like what you find."

"I'm sure. Thanks for the info and the box. I'll bring it back when I'm done." Aubrey walked away with the single carton and a renewed sense of purpose. *I'll find this murderer, no matter how long it takes.*

Aubrey took the Banker's box to a small room with a table. She spread out a couple of the bags as she reviewed their contents. She pulled out the bag with Lori's clothes, compared them with the forensics report. Everything was accurate. The baggie with the glass fragments was still confusing, though. *Huh, what is that? Looks like a partial word or number.* Aubrey found a magnifying glass and tried to discern what the letter was.

Looks like an R or maybe a B. Aubrey wrote a note to check into what kinds of fragile glass has letters on it. *Reminds me of test tube glass.* She considered whether it could be a broken light bulb, but dismissed the idea. It didn't really look like one, didn't have the right type of curve to the shape. She examined the other fragments and found no other writing or numbers. She couldn't recall seeing anything in the binder about a piece of glass with a letter on it. She'd have to double-check. She was running out of time, so she put everything back in the box and returned it to Sergeant Piper.

As Aubrey walked over to the Personnel Department to request Detective Rollins' records, she recalled how gentle and considerate he was. He never pressured Aubrey but instead, coaxed memories from her. She shared with him how she and Lori would play explorer in the park, tracking animals from the footprints. Aubrey laughed. They never found any of the animals but had so much fun trying, she'd never forget her best friend. Lori was always willing to try anything Aubrey thought up for them to do. How would she ever find another like her?

Aubrey pushed through the doors of the Personnel Office and pushed away her memories. *I have to focus on finding the scumbag who did this to Lori.* She wasn't sure if she should call first or merely show up, but she wanted to have the address and phone number, regardless of how she chose to make contact with him.

Gladys, the records clerk, was a middle-aged woman with an old-fashioned, graying beehive hairdo. Her reading glasses, strung around her neck on a chain, sat on her yellow and red floral dress. Aubrey had always liked her. She cracked her gum and told Aubrey, "You have to fill out this form first, so we have a record of anyone requesting personal information on an officer. Since he's retired and you're an active-duty officer, it shouldn't be a problem. We'll also need to know why you want it."

"Thanks, Gladys, no problem. I'm reviewing a cold case he investigated," Aubrey explained, as she completed the form. "I'm hoping he knows more than what's in the book." She smiled. "Hey, new perfume? Smells nice."

"Thanks. Yes, it is." Gladys grinned as her fingers played with her glasses, and she blushed at the compliment. "Well, good luck, girl, I hope you're right. Wait a minute, let me find it for you."

She left to look for the retired detective's file as Aubrey waited by the desk. She hoped Rollins would still be in the city. A few minutes later, Gladys returned with a piece of paper in her hand.

"Here ya go, honey. Hope he can help." Gladys handed her the slip of paper.

Aubrey was pleased to see he was living nearby. She needed to get moving, or she'd be late for her shift, but at least she had a place to start. She put the note in her jeans pocket, thanked Gladys, and hurried to the restroom to change into her uniform. She'd learned to put her personal clothing back in her car while she worked, but she continued to wish for a women's locker room. She believed it was only a matter of time before there would be more female officers here.

Aubrey was singled out during Roll Call for her apprehension of the convenience store thief and received a round of applause. She blushed at the praise but was pleased her work was recognized.

After Mills had reviewed all pertinent information to the group of officers gathered, Aubrey headed out of the Squad Room toward the parking lot to pick up her patrol car, Scott Fuller blocked her path. Despite a year having passed, Fuller's bullying toward Aubrey had continued, so she was wary as he advanced closer.

"Hey, baby, how's it going?" he asked with a sneer. "Think you're pretty hot stuff 'cuz you caught that idiot at the convenience store?"

"I was doing my job and happened to be in the right place at the right time," Aubrey replied in her best cop voice. "What do you care, anyway?" *Why do I even bother talking to him? I don't need to explain myself to this jerk.*

Fuller drew nearer, invading her personal space. Aubrey refused to retreat or show him any reaction. She could smell his mouthwash mixed with coffee on his breath. A whiff of his cologne, an earthy, fresh scent, assaulted her nose. *I love his cologne ... but nothing can cover up his disgusting behavior.* As he leaned in closer, she instinctively put her hand up to force him back. He laughed and retreated.

"What do you think I'm going to do?" he taunted.

"Nothing, if I can help it. Leave me alone. I have to get on patrol." Aubrey glared at him. She attempted to move past him, but he put his arm across the doorway, barring her exit.

They were the last two in the squad room. She crossed her arms over her chest, raised her eyebrows at his juvenile behavior, and waited. *What is with you, asshole?*

Fuller snorted, removed his arm, and sauntered toward the parking lot. Aubrey hated he could sense her anxiety around him, and he played on her discomfort every time. She couldn't seem to control her nervousness. If she were sitting when he approached, her leg would bounce; if standing, she clenched her fists until her nails dug into her palm, sometimes drawing blood. She shuddered, the residue of his rage engulfing her in an unwelcome embrace.

She would need to find a better way to handle him.

****

"What do I have to do to make her quit? It's been two years since we started the academy together. I've tried physically intimidating her, switched her uniforms the first day, which was fun, making her look ridiculous." Fuller spoke to himself as he started his car and laughed out loud at the image of Aubrey in her too-large uniform. "She just won't give up. Now, she's the 'hero' because she caught a two-penny, wanna-be crook. I don't know how much more of her I can take." He ground his teeth as he used a black marker to obliterate the picture of her in the newspaper article about the attempted store robbery, then tossed the paper in the trash.

Chapter 3

Patrol was slow. Teenagers loitering around a party store skedaddled when they saw Aubrey show up. She handled a minor fender-bender between a student leaving the school's parking lot, and Miss Olsen, her former Spanish teacher. When her shift ended, she changed into her civilian clothes and left for home.

Halfway to her place, Aubrey snatched her courage and stopped at Detective Rollins's address to see if he would talk to her. *He might not even be here, but it's worth a try.* She found the street and parked in front of his house. The lights and TV were on. She stepped out of her car and walked to the door.

As she prepared to knock, the door opened. Retired Detective Steve Rollins was dressed in khaki pants and a navy polo shirt, his lived-in and weathered face disguised his dimples when he smiled. He looked the same as she remembered, except for a smattering of grey hair at his temples and a few unruly tufts.

"Well, well, well, if it isn't Officer Aubrey Stanton. Have you come to arrest me?" he teased.

"I don't think so. Have you done anything wrong, sir?" Her mouth turned upward into a warm and open smile, belying her nervousness.

"So good to see you, Aubrey. I'm glad you stopped by. Come on in." Rollins opened the door for her to enter. "Gosh, it's been, what, about ten years since the last time we talked? Your mother finally told me, in no uncertain terms, to leave you alone. So I did."

He pressed his lips together in a resigned smile. "I knew you wouldn't know anything different, but I liked seeing and chatting with you. I had three sons, no daughters, so I enjoyed watching you grow up. I respected your mother's wishes, though, and quit dropping by."

His face brightened. "I did go to your graduation from the academy, but you were surrounded by your friends, so I didn't want to bother you." He tilted his head toward the kitchen. "Can I get you something to drink? I seem to remember you liked chocolate Yoo-Hoo, right?"

A laugh escaped her lips at the unexpected memory. "You're right, I did. But I've moved on to other things. If you have a cola, I'll take one, thanks. I wish you'd've said hello after the ceremony, it *has* been a long time. I always enjoyed seeing you, too, even if the reason was unpleasant, *you* never were."

Rollins turned off the TV and went to the kitchen to get the drinks. He brought Aubrey a can of cola and one for himself. "Thanks. And to what do I owe the pleasure of this visit from my favorite witness?"

"Well, sir, I decided it was time to find the person who killed my friend. I know you did everything you could, but I'd like to ask you a few questions if it's all right?"

"Aubrey, first of all, now we're both adults, and you *are* a police officer, please call me Steve." He gestured toward the sofa and continued, "Here, take a seat. You know I *did* do everything I could to find her killer before I retired. I followed every lead, every suggestion, every anonymous phone call that came in." He threw up his hands in frustration.

"There was nothing more I could do but let her lie in peace. I hoped a more skilled detective than I would attempt to solve it. I even delayed my retirement and reviewed every note written, to be sure I had covered all the bases. I'm not sure there's anything I can tell you that's not already in the file. You're welcome to ask, though." Rollins settled himself in his worn, but sturdy armchair, opposite from Aubrey on the soft leather sofa, who fingered the brightly colored pillow next to her.

"Thank you, S..S..Steve," she stuttered, uncomfortable with the new familiarity. "Yeah, this might take a while to get used to. I'm certain I'm not more skilled than you, but there are new technologies I can use to bring the murderer to justice. I *do* know you worked relentlessly on solving this crime. I remember your visits to the house. I always felt guilty I didn't have more information for you."

She took a sip from the soda can and set it on a coaster on the end table. "I asked so many questions of my friends and classmates over the years, most quit talking to me. I know it's foolish, but I feel responsible. She was my best friend, and I sent her on ahead that day, so I could earn brownie points with my teacher. I need to do what I can to find the person who did it."

"I understand, but remember you're *not* responsible. The person who did it, is responsible." He took a deep breath and let it out. "Okay. Go ahead with your questions. I'll tell you anything I know."

"Great. Thanks. I reviewed the autopsy report and saw the techs recovered hair and glass fragments. Did anyone follow up on them? I didn't see anything in the book." Aubrey took another swig of her cola, holding the can to keep her hands steady.

"Hair samples are hard to identify. Except for length or color, there's not much to go on. We looked at the known criminals in the area, even her parents, although I never considered them suspects. None of them matched. The glass fragments were always a mystery to me, but they were fragments and could have come from anywhere."

He sat back and stroked his chin. "The glass was fragile, though, and looked to me like a broken test tube. You know, like the kind from a chemistry lab. We checked the local pharmacy and the high school to see if anyone had taken tubes from their storage, but they said it didn't look like it. Neither had an up-to-date inventory at the time, so they might not have missed one or two anyway."

"I thought the same thing about the glass being test tube fragments. Were there any known sexual predators in the city you know of?"

"Yes, Aubrey, there were a few, but there's no central listing of them to check. We had to either *know* who they were from having arrested them previously or ask other nearby departments who they had on *their* radar. A state listing would be nice, but I don't see it happening any time soon."

He shook his head and sighed. "There were a lot of dead ends, no pun intended. Everyone working on the case was frustrated by the lack of leads. Murders were less common in those days than they are now. Even the fingerprints we found on the knife —"

Aubrey sat up. "The knife? I didn't realize you'd found a knife. I must have missed it when I read the chronological report. I didn't have time today to go through the whole box."

"We found it much later during a search at another, unrelated crime scene in the park, over by the playground. The killer must have dropped it. I don't know if it was intentional or accidental, but being on the other side of the park, I guessed he'd left it there. It was somewhat buried. I believe he thought we wouldn't connect it. It was a generic fixed-blade, six-inch-long hunting knife. We knew it was from Lori's case because we were able to have the blood residue on it typed. Lori had a rare blood type—AB Negative, so we knew it was the one we had been looking for. It also matched the wounds on her.

"Another officer was supposed to update the book with the information. Maybe he didn't. It happens. It should be in the box though, for all the good it will do you. We ran the fingerprints through our database, but if the guy hadn't ever been fingerprinted, or came from out of the area, we wouldn't have been able to match them to anything. We would have needed a suspect to compare with, and we never had one. I understand the FBI is starting to put together a nationwide fingerprint system, which will be great when they finish it."

"Okay, I understand. If I find a suspect, at least I'll have prints to work with."

Rollins smiled at her. "I'm guessing you want to be a detective, like me? Is that what this is all about?"

Aubrey blushed and dipped her head. "Yes. But, I made a promise to Lori to find her killer, and I plan to do my best to make it happen. I appreciate you talking to me, and I don't want to take up any more of your time."

Aubrey stood up and put her hand out to shake his, but he pulled her into his arms and hugged her tightly. "I wish you the best, Aubrey. I'm very proud of you. You were a smart and brave little girl, and I see you're an intelligent and courageous woman now. I hope you do find out who killed your friend, but remember, there are plenty of other people who need your help who are still here."

He released her and said, "Again, I'm so glad you came over. It's good to see you. Feel free to stop by any time. I don't have much to do these days, so if I can be of any help, don't hesitate to ask, okay?"

"I will. Thanks again." Aubrey turned away and walked to her car, tears forming in her eyes. No one had ever called her smart or courageous before, and it took a few moments to pull herself together before she could head toward home.

****

Kizzy greeted Aubrey at the door, panting, yipping and jumping as best as her tired, arthritic legs would allow. Aubrey wrinkled her nose, detected the smell of urine, and knew Kizzy hadn't made it outside through her pet door, again. *Par for the course. Kizzy's getting too old to be left alone all day. I'll need to take her back to the vet and have her kidneys checked.*

She rubbed Kizzy's belly. "How's my best girl doing today? Did you enjoy the new bone I got you?"

Kizzy responded to Aubrey's attention with wet, doggy kisses and butt wiggles.

"Hey, you're drowning me with your tongue."

Aubrey teased her but was thrilled Kizzy had lived this long. Thirteen years was old for a terrier, and she knew the end was coming. The thought of losing her best friend saddened her. Aubrey refilled Kizzy's water and kibble bowls. She let the little dog outside in the backyard to do her business and went hunting for the accident. She found it in the bathroom, *appropriate place, anyway,* cleaned it up, and walked back out to the kitchen.

Aubrey opened the refrigerator, looking for any leftovers to re-warm for dinner. A container of stuffed shells sat in a bottom bin, and she pulled the dish out. Opening the top, she saw green mold on the cheese topping and dumped the whole thing in the trash. *Oh well, it was a good thought. Now I have to find something fast and easy to eat instead.*

After downing two peanut-butter-and-jelly sandwiches and some chips, Aubrey cleaned the kitchen and played with Kizzy for a while.

"I think I'll give your Uncle Tom a call," she told the dog. Kizzy panted at her.

As she picked up the phone, she recalled he was three hours behind her. It would be about five p.m. there, and he might still be at work. She'd try him there first.

"Hello?" Tom answered.

"Hey, Tom, it's Aubrey. Have you got a minute?"

"Sure. This is a surprise. What's up? I hope it's long-winded since it's like, five o'clock, and I'm trying to get out of here."

"Sorry, I forgot. Should I call you later after you get home?"

"Nah. It's okay, just giving you a hard time."

"Ha, ha. Thanks. I have a question for you. I'm going back over the evidence files on my friend, Lori. Remember when I found her in the park?"

"Of course. I'll never forget. But why are you looking into it now? I thought they gave up on her case a long time ago?"

Aubrey heard a touch of wariness in Tom's voice. She hesitated a moment before saying, "Well, they did, but I thought I'd see if I could find out more about what happened to her. I pulled the evidence box and the murder book. The autopsy showed they'd recovered glass fragments, and I found them in one of the evidence bags. The pieces are tiny, and they seem very fragile. One has a white letter on it, looks like an 'R' or a 'B.' Detective Rollins thought perhaps it could be from a test tube. What do you think?"

"I have no idea without seeing it. Can you send me a closeup picture?"

"I don't know. It might too small to photograph with my Polaroid. You work with test tubes. Can you look at yours and see if the idea sounds possible?"

"I work with *beakers*, Squirt, not test tubes, but I'll look. I'll have to get back to you."

Aubrey grinned at the old nickname. "Fine. I'll get a photo in the mail to you, and you can let me know after you've had a chance to check, okay?"

"Of course."

"Hey, I've meant to ask you since I first became a cop, what about your other job, the county coroner?" Aubrey knew her brother loved to lecture and share his knowledge with anyone who would listen.

Tom laughed, "I don't want to say being a coroner was more *fun,* exactly, but I can say I enjoyed it. Since I was the only one in town who had taken a pre-med course, the townspeople figured I had more knowledge than they did. So, they elected me to take over when the previous coroner left town. I was paid twenty-five dollars a month."

"Really? Why would you do that, especially for so little pay?" Mya asked.

"I enjoyed it, and I made plenty of money at the mill. Generally, when someone did something stupid, like trying to walk across one of the rivers, stepping on the algae-covered stones, and losing their balance, they died from hypothermia in the freezing cold mountain runoff. Sometimes they would hike up the slippery mountain slopes and break their necks in a fall. It was my job to pronounce them dead, once they were found. Afterward, they were sent out to the medical examiner in Redding for the autopsy."

"Oh, okay, I was curious and thought your knowledge could come in handy one day for me."

"Sure, if I can ever help, I'm happy to." He paused, and Aubrey waited to hear his thoughts. "Sorry I didn't make your graduation ceremony last year. Did Mom or Dad go?"

"It's fine. No, neither of them could come, but my friends were there, and I understand how hard it would have been for you. Talk to you soon."

"Will do." As Tom was hanging up the phone, Aubrey heard him mutter, "Why on earth did she decide to reopen that old wound?"

Interesting. Why should Tom care if I'm looking into it? Maybe he's worried about me, although that would be a first.

Aubrey turned on her cassette player with a tape of her favorite artist, Carly Simon, and reviewed the notes she'd taken earlier. A couple of hours later, her thoughts were spiraling. She needed a break, so she pulled out the book she'd been reading, *Crocodile on the Sandbank* by Elizabeth Peters, and curled up in her ancient leather armchair to read for a while.

When she started yawning, she completed her nightly ritual and climbed into bed. She reviewed her day and tried to sleep but tossed and turned most of the night. Something nagged at the back of her brain, but she couldn't quite grasp it. It felt like a dream on waking, not remembering the critical parts as it whirled and dissipated into vapor. She knew it was crucial, but try as she might, nothing would come.

She finally drifted off to sleep, only a few hours before her alarm would sound.

Aubrey was walking through the woods, Kizzy jumping around her feet. An adult version of Lori stood before her, staring with scarlet eyes, blood crusted on her chest, and her hair disheveled, with bits of leaves sticking out. She wore a decaying, faded, Brownie uniform. Lori pointed a chewed-off finger at Aubrey.

"You know who did this, Aubrey. Find him for me. Please."

Aubrey jolted awake. She sat up, heart pounding, and shook her head. *It was a dream. The pictures I'd been looking at today must've seared into my brain.* She lay back down, and a few minutes later fell into a restless sleep with Kizzy snuggled by her side.

When her alarm clanged, Aubrey still felt groggy and tried to patiently wait for her coffee to brew. She'd need it today. The dream image of Lori continued to haunt her, and she wondered if her subconscious knew something she had overlooked. She would think about it later, she had a busy day ahead.

Sergeant Mills had chosen Aubrey to visit the high school for Career Day, and she wanted to make sure she represented the department well. After her first day fiasco with her uniform, she'd always brought it home but changed in the restroom at the station.

Aubrey found a note in her jeans pocket that day a year ago, telling her to return the ill-fitting uniforms and shoes to the Quartermaster and request the correct size. She still had to have them tailored, but not immediately, as the new ones fit better. She never found out who left the note but was grateful, regardless.

This morning, Aubrey'd paid extra attention to her uniform and polished her shoes and shield until they shone. She'd rehearsed her ten-minute speech for hours so she wouldn't forget anything.

She adored her career and was determined to make a good impression. Aubrey was excited to let the teenage girls hear how fulfilling the job was, as well as how much fun it could be. The police officers were her family, if not by blood, by camaraderie, and she knew another cop always had her back. The pay was no great shakes but enough to live on.

She drank a cup of coffee, bolted down two scrambled eggs, fed and watered Kizzy, and sprinted out to her car.

Aubrey had kept one promise to herself. She'd always admired her childhood neighbor, Mrs. Thomas, a single, independent woman with three children. She was the only one Aubrey knew in the neighborhood who worked. Mrs. Thomas had a yellow Chevy Impala when Aubrey was growing up.

To Aubrey, it signified the freedom and individuality she craved. Although Aubrey's wasn't the same make, model, or year, she'd bought a used, bright yellow, 1966 Ford Mustang. Wherever she traveled in her sports car, she felt wild and free. She slid in, buckled up, backed out of her driveway, and sped off to the school.

Chapter 4

Aubrey pulled into the Spencer High School parking lot. She recalled, without a hint of nostalgia, dreading every day there. The other students considered her strange. Her goal of joining the police department, along with weight training and self-defense courses, set her apart from the girls who worried about invitations to the prom or football games.

No one asked Aubrey to those social events. It stung the next day as she was left out of the gossip about parties and other news. Most of the kids she'd known had had no clue what they wanted after graduation; college for a few, marriage for others, the boys were the only ones who considered getting a job. She consoled herself with always knowing her goal in life.

She stepped out of her patrol car and noted the curious looks from several students as she made her way to the front office. She hadn't been inside the school since she'd left it three years before. *Interesting how certain things never change, while all around, everything else does.* She walked down the hall and checked out the posters and bulletins on the walls, watched the students hurrying to class. She smiled at a few of the girls, who turned away, giggling, most likely at her uniform.

As Aubrey opened the door to the office, Miss Olsen came out, and they nearly collided with each other. Aubrey held the door open, supporting her former teacher by her arm, and stood in the doorway as Miss Olsen regained her balance. Miss Olsen was five-foot-nothing, white-haired with wire-rim glasses, and always had a kind word for everyone. She was Aubrey's favorite teacher.

"Oh, Aubrey!" She covered her mouth and corrected herself. "Oops, I mean, Officer Stanton, how nice to see you again."

"Hola, Señora Olsen, Aubrey is fine. How are you doing? Did you get your car fixed after the incident in the parking lot?"

"Oh, goodness, wasn't that a mess! Yes, I did get it fixed, but it cost me a deductible. They said it was because the accident was on private property. The parking lot, I guess. Thank you for your help. Good to know you still remember some Spanish from my class." She winked at Aubrey.

"It was my pleasure. I'm sorry to hear it cost you money, though. The kids aren't very observant when they're in a hurry to leave, are they?" She chuckled. "I'm here for career day. Should I see Mrs. Fraser at the desk?"

"Yes, she can tell you where to wait while they get started. Take care. Adiós." She patted Aubrey's arm and walked off with a little wave.

Aubrey turned toward the front desk and stood back from the bevy of activity, as students and teachers started their day. Mrs. Fraser looked up and gave Aubrey a tight-lipped smirk. She cocked her head and looked sideways toward a frantic teen attempting to find a parental note in her seemingly bottomless backpack.

She motioned to Aubrey to step up and asked her, "You're here for Career Day, right?" Without waiting for an answer, she said, "Speakers are meeting behind the stage in the auditorium if you'd like to head over there. Thanks for coming. We've had two calls from people canceling. I hope there aren't anymore, or you may be the whole show. I hope you prepared for a longer speech?" At Aubrey's horrified expression, she laughed and said, "No, I'm kidding. We'll figure it out. Have fun."

"Thanks, Mrs. Fraser. It looks like you're having fun already." Aubrey grinned at the harried office fixture, glad she still managed to wrangle students with ease. The secretary had been at Spencer High forever but was still spry and shrewd.

Aubrey headed down the hallway toward the auditorium, wondering who else would be there and whether she'd know them. The bell rang as the last of the students and teachers disappeared into various classrooms and closed doors.

The auditorium door was open. Aubrey walked in, looked around, and took a deep breath. A familiar mixture of smells assaulted her nose. It reminded her of dirty feet, disinfectant, and an unknown aroma specific to the room. The odor pulled her memory back to school concerts, plays, and boring assemblies. It also reminded her of taunts and having her chair-back repeatedly kicked, the stares, the whispers, and all her distant self-doubts.

The seats, arranged stadium-style, had dull red, worn-out cushions with black checks, the armrests were gouged, inked and dirty, several had bits of stuffing sticking out of the seams. Aubrey never understood why they carpeted the floor since it was impossible to keep clean and smelled like a wet dog.

"So, Aubrey, they also invited you to speak to the hormone-driven, insecure, and arrogant senior class?" asked a memorable voice behind her.

Aubrey turned, and Brad Davis, from the graduating class before hers, stood grinning at her. She hadn't realized he knew her name.

"Oh. Hi, Brad. I'm glad to see a familiar face. I'm surprised you recognized me."

He smiled a warm, genuinely-pleased-to-see-her smile. "Of course, I would. You were the only girl I've ever known who could bench press a hundred-and-thirty pounds and make it look easy. All your working out must come in handy with your chosen profession. I wondered if you'd gone through with becoming a cop. I'm glad to see you, too."

"Are you still in town? What are you doing now?" Aubrey asked, to shift the conversation away from herself.

"I moved over to Mill's Creek after high school and graduated from Michigan State with a degree in International Relations. I'll apply to Law School, but have to take my LSAT next month first." The boyish grin Aubrey always loved, spread across his face.

"Wow. Well, good luck. Are you here to talk about international relations or the law? Defense or prosecutor?"

"Thanks. I'm thinking prosecutor right now, but haven't really decided yet. Oh, hey, there's Sam. Do you remember him? He's a little older than us, but I guess he's running the show today. Let's go up."

"No, I don't know him. I'll follow you."

Sam greeted them on the stairs to the right of the stage. "Hi, thanks so much for coming. How's it going, Brad? And you're Aubrey Stanton, correct? I'm Sam North, I'm one of the guidance counselors here. I believe I graduated the year you were a freshman."

"Hi, Sam, nice to meet you. Yes, I'm Aubrey, and please don't remind me of my freshman year." She grimaced and rolled her eyes. "Is there anyone else coming I might know?"

"I invited John Curry to talk about being a doctor, and Lisa Jameson, who's an airline stewardess married to a pilot, who may come with her as well. Also, Dave Wright, a local vet

... Phil Griffin, who's a mechanic, and our own Miss Olsen to talk about her life as a teacher. Do you know any of them?"

"Well, I know Miss Olsen, of course, and Phil and Lisa. Don't know the others. Do you, Brad?"

"Actually, besides you, Aubrey, I only know Dave. I take my dog, Bubba, to him."

Sam's face brightened as the door in the back of the room opened. "Here come the others now ... come on up on stage, folks. Thanks for coming."

As the newcomers arrived on stage, everyone introduced themselves and greeted each other. Aubrey was curious as to how Lisa would react to her. They were not friendly during their school days together, but Lisa was pleasant, and Aubrey was happy for her. Lisa's husband couldn't make it, but they had plenty of people to speak to the students. Any more, and it would be hard to keep the kids' attention.

****

After each of the speakers had completed the synopsis of their career choice, Sam opened the floor to questions. Most of the students acted bored, but a few asked reasonably intelligent questions, interested in learning more. A couple said they were disappointed there were no military recruiters included, and others, fidgeting in their seats, clearly itched to leave.

Aubrey felt her presentation had gone as well as could be expected. She received a couple of basic questions from one of the boys about the academy and whether he would be required to have a degree. The girls whispered and giggled during her carefully prepared speech. It disappointed her she hadn't sounded more enticing to those in attendance. Maybe in time, things would change.

When the students had disbursed to their respective classes, Brad stopped Aubrey as she was getting ready to leave.

"Hey, Aubrey, would you have time to go for coffee, before you go back to work?" He looked at her with his eyebrows raised in a question. His cologne evoked raw sensuality with its expensive patchouli, leather, and bergamot scent.

I could stand here all day, simply smelling him. Get a grip, Stanton. She took a deep breath before responding. "Gosh, Brad, I'd like to, but I really have to get back. I get off at four o'clock, though, if you'd like to get something?"

"Yeah, sure. Let me give you my number in case something comes up, and you can't make it. Police work can be unpredictable, right?"

Aubrey grinned. "Yes, it can be, but usually not here. It's a pretty quiet town. How about we meet at Sparky's Grill on Main Street at four-thirty? It'll give me time to change out of my work clothes."

"Great! See you. Good job today. I enjoyed your presentation, even though it looked like the female students might not have. But you never know who might have been listening and didn't want to draw attention to themselves. Kids can be cruel."

"Thanks. You're right. Yours was interesting, too, and the kids were curious, at least. See you later."

Aubrey considered Brad as she drove to the police station. *Hmmm, that was unexpected. Pleasantly so, though. When we were in school, I didn't think he knew I existed. Maybe it's time I got to know him a little better.*

Chapter 5

After her shift, Aubrey dropped off her weekly report to Sergeant Mills. It contained almost nothing since she'd barely begun her investigation. But she promised him a summary of what she was exploring each week, so she turned it in faithfully.

Aubrey changed into jeans, a fresh T-shirt, and tennis shoes. She looked into the cheap, hazy mirror, and wondered, *What can I do with this hair? Since it's been in a ponytail all day, I can't take it out ... I can't take a shower... screw it. I'll leave it alone, nothing else I can do. I can* put *a little makeup on, though. Can't hurt to try to look as good as possible.*

Aubrey made herself presentable and walked to the parking lot. She slipped into the black leather, bucket seat, and smiled. *It's been a while since I had dinner with an interesting man. I'm looking forward to seeing Brad again.*

She drove home first, took care of Kizzy, and headed to Sparky's Grill. As she pulled into the parking lot, she saw Brad waiting outside the restaurant. *That's a good sign. He's on time.* She turned off the engine, stepped out of her car, and met him at the door.

"Hi, again. Nice car," Brad said. "How was the rest of your day?"

"Thanks. Typical, nothing exciting. What did you do?"

"I took Bubba for a long walk and a romp around Spencer Park. He loves the undeveloped space. There's not much left in the city, is there?"

Chagrined, Aubrey replied, "Yeah, I used to love the park, and even though it's been a long time, I can't bring myself to take my dog, Kizzy, into those areas."

"Oh, God, I'm sorry. I shouldn't have brought it up. I forgot it's where you found that poor girl." His face reddened.

"I know it's been ages, but I'm looking into her murder, so it's brought back all the bad feelings. Not your fault. Let's go in and get a table."

"Right. Yes. Let's."

Sparky's Grill was a Spencer staple. It had been there as long as the town itself. It offered the usual fare of sandwiches, burgers, fries, and had a liquor license. The décor had changed two years ago, from off-kilter tables and worn-out chairs to forest green bench seats and booths. The walls still looked freshly painted in a creamy white eggshell, and photos, framed in oak with green mats, of the town since its beginning, adorned the walls. Comfortable, clean, and the food wasn't bad either.

The restaurant hostess, dressed in a miniskirt and low cut blouse, seated them at a table near the back by a window, handed them menus, and put down glasses of water. "Your server will be right with you." She returned to her station.

"I'm surprised they let her dress like that," Aubrey said, eyes wide.

"I agree. Her skirt's a bit short, isn't it? Maybe the owner discovered if she dresses like that, it brings in more customers … the drinking, spending kind."

"Yeah, maybe. If you give a guy enough to drink, he forgets how much money he's spent."

"Oh well. It really is good to see you again, Aubrey. Since I've been at school for the past four years, I lost touch with many of my old friends, who have all gone their separate ways. I haven't made many new ones, either ... until now. I hope." He grinned.

Aubrey found the nervous touching of his hair and shirt endearing. She had to stop herself from continually grinning like an idiot. At the academy, she was trained in the reading of basic body language but hadn't quite mastered controlling her own tics and tells.

A young woman approached their table, and as Brad pulled his eyes away from Aubrey and shifted his body, his hand knocked over the glass of water on the table. They both jumped up.

"Hi guys, I'm Jenny. Why don't I move you to the next table over, and we'll get this cleaned up? Don't worry about it. Happens all the time. Can I get you something else to drink?"

"I'll have a cola, please," said Aubrey, as they settled themselves at the new table.

"Me, too," said Brad, his face red.

Jenny walked away to get their drink orders. They overheard her yell for the busboy to clean up the spill.

"Ok, that was stupid. I'm sorry. I guess I'm nervous. I haven't dated much in the past couple of years, and I'm out of practice." Brad fidgeted as he apologized.

"It's okay. It was only water." *Good to know I'm not the only one nervous here.*

"Do you want to order dinner? You've had a long day." He leaned forward.

Aubrey hesitated but grinned. "Yeah, sure. It'll give us more time to talk."

Two hours later, Aubrey and Brad had eaten hamburgers and fries ... hers well-done, his medium-rare ... drank loads of cola, laughed, and talked about mutual friends, their old teachers, and college experiences.

"I better get going, Brad," she said. "I had fun tonight."

"Me, too. Um, could I see you again?"

Her eyes lit up as she answered, "Sure, I'd like to see you, also." She scribbled her number on a napkin. "I don't usually give out my personal number, I'm sure you know why. But I'll give it to you if you promise not to share it. You know if you do, I'll have to kill you, right?" They laughed at the old joke. "I gotta go. Kizzy's waiting for me, and most likely, Bubba is waiting for you, too."

"Don't worry, I won't share this with anyone. I'll call you soon. Good night." He leaned in for what she thought was going to be a kiss but instead turned into a hug that she happily provided.

"Night, Brad." Aubrey climbed into her car, and with a final wave, drove home, a goofy grin on her face. *I hope he calls. We got along pretty well, and he's fun. I guess we'll see.*

****

Tom called the next evening. After a few minutes of chatting, he said, "I got your letter with the pictures of the piece of glass you asked about. I checked it out under one of our high-powered microscopes because the photo details were hard to see, and it was a bit blurry. It's definitely the letter 'P.' My guess is it's from a Pyrex tube. They've been around forever, and most other test tubes have numbers, lines, ml, or a C. Pyrex is relatively common."

"Oh, okay. I appreciate you taking the time to look at it. Sorry I can't talk longer, I'm in the middle of something. I'll catch up with you soon."

"No trouble. Let's not wait two years again, okay? Have a good night."

"Thanks. You, too."

Darn it. I wanted it to be a better clue. I knew it wouldn't be easy, but this is a letdown. Aubrey returned to her notes, drawings, and ideas sprawled across the kitchen table. Picking up her copy of the Murder Book, she took a deep breath and opened it once more to the first page.

I need to review everything again. I'd depended too much on that piece of glass solving everything. How naïve am I? Now I have more questions.

She jotted down her thoughts. *Doctors, lab people, students, teachers, researchers, chemists. Anyone else? Hmm, I'll have to think about it. Of course, the glass could've been on the ground, broken by who-knows-who a year before!*

She shut the book, pinched the bridge of her nose and sat back in the chair. It was past midnight, and her head ached. Her muscles had relaxed into the soft chair when Kizzy growled. Aubrey heard a noise from the garage and bolted out of her chair. Kizzy rarely growled. They were both on full alert.

"Shh, Kizzy. Stay," she whispered to the dog. She glided down the hallway to her bedroom and grabbed her off-duty weapon from the nightstand. She clutched her gun and heard Kizzy barking her most fierce, get-out-of-here warning. The rattling, scratching, and bumps sounded like someone trying to open the service door between the house and the garage.

Holding her handgun at face level, she sidled up to the side of the door, grabbed the handle and flung it open.

The largest raccoon Aubrey had ever seen, tumbled inside. It looked astonished to find itself inside and frantically searched for the way out. Its body was so rotund, it scrabbled to get its bearings again as Kizzy lunged at the strange ball of brown and grey fur.

"No, Kizzy. Stop!" she shouted, grabbing at and missing the dog's collar.

Kizzy ran under the table, low-growling, and whimpering.

Aubrey set her gun down on the table. "Let's get you back outside where you belong."

A broom was leaning on the kitchen wall, so she used it to whack the reluctant beast back into the garage. She followed it out, giving it motivation when it dawdled and saw the small side door was open. She remembered the lock didn't always catch. *I must not have slammed it hard enough the last time.* Once the fat raccoon was safely outdoors, she secured the access door.

Her heart settled into a normal rhythm when she saw Kizzy lying on the kitchen floor, bleeding and whining. Aubrey ran to get a towel, wrapped her friend in it, and examined the wounds. The little dog looked at her owner with weepy eyes. One deep wound would require stitches, but the others were superficial.

"Oh, poor baby. Let me call the vet. You'll be all right." Aubrey petted Kizzy's head as she dialed the vet's office number.

"Dr. Kirby's answering service. How can I help you?" said an officious, tired-sounding, and not particularly friendly, voice.

Aubrey'd forgotten how late it was. "This is Aubrey Stanton. My dog was bitten or clawed by a raccoon tonight. One of the wounds is deep, and I'd like the doc to look at it."

"Please hold, and I'll try to reach him."

The three-minute wait felt like a lifetime before the woman returned to the phone, "Dr. Kirby said for you to bring the dog in immediately. He'll meet you at his office."

"Great. Thanks." She hung up the phone and bundled Kizzy into the car.

Aubrey drove at break-neck speed to the vet's office cradling Kizzy in her lap. She parked in front, gently lifted Kizzy out of the car and carried her into the building.

Doctor Kirby met her in the lobby with disheveled hair and eyes half-closed. He was dressed in what appeared to be hastily donned jeans, a misbuttoned red plaid shirt, and two different colored socks. At least his sneakers matched, even if the laces weren't tied.

"Aubrey, bring her into the exam room and let me take a look."

She followed him into a brightly-lit room with a stainless steel table, a small counter, and sink. She set a whining Kizzy on the table. Test tubes stood on the countertop, and she made a mental note to ask about them another time.

"So, how did our girl tangle with a raccoon?"

"She started growling, and I heard noises in the garage. Sounded like a burglar trying to break into the house. I opened the door between the house and the garage, and a big ol' raccoon fell right inside. Kizzy was angry about the intrusion and confronted the little robber, like the excellent mini police dog she is, but came away with these bites and scratches."

"You were right to call. This one is deep. I'll need to sedate her a bit to clean it out properly and stitch it. The other wounds need cleaning. I'll give you antibiotics for her. Did the raccoon act rabid ... kind of crazy or foaming at the mouth?"

"No. Actually, it looked confused, but more than ready to get away from my little terror with teeth."

Ninety minutes later, Aubrey and Kizzy arrived home. Still recovering from the sedation, the dog slept. Aubrey put one of the dog's little shirts on her to prevent any chewing at the stitches. She'd found the shirt preferable to a cone, and it worked as well. Kizzy tolerated it.

Aubrey settled her sleepy friend in bed and finally herself. With her alarm set for five o'clock, the day would arrive earlier than usual.

Chapter 6

On Friday, a rash of petty crimes kept Aubrey busy at work, and she made no progress on Lori's murder. On Saturday, usually her day off, she agreed to fill in on the night shift for one of the guys on vacation.

The nearby Pontiac Silverdome hosted a Led Zepplin music concert, the largest indoor performance to date. The band showed up via helicopter ninety minutes late and made everyone wait for them. Their music topped music charts, but the concert also topped local law enforcement charts with fans fighting, smoking weed, underage drinking, and other minor crimes. The city police requested back-up from nearby departments after watching the crowd's unruly behavior.

The sergeant issued orders to Aubrey and her fellow officers who were gathered in the station. "Stanton, Fuller, Edwards, Johnson, you're going to Pontiac to help with those crazy fans at the stadium." Sergeant Mills mopped his brow and snarled, "Dispatch says it's getting too much for the locals to handle. Take your riot gear, you never know what might happen."

"Yes, sir," the four responded in unison. They left the squad room to pick up the necessary items to stow in their individual patrol cars and convoy the fifteen minutes to the venue.

One of the lessons Aubrey'd learned during her first month on the job was to make sure she was taken seriously. She knew her gender made her appear to be an easier target than her male counterparts and could relax only after she was able to assess any potential threats. One night, Aubrey and FTO McLain had responded to a rowdy party and, upon arrival, saw a couple male underage teens sitting on the front porch drinking beer. They walked up to the boys and told them to dump out their cans.

The boy on the lowest step handed his drink to Aubrey, who had her long, heavy, tactical flashlight positioned between her side and her upper arm. When she leaned down to take his beer, the flashlight tilted downward and whacked the kid on the head. Not hard and not intentionally, but the boy took exception to being struck, jumped up, and pushed her into the bushes. McLain grabbed the boy and handcuffed him before Aubrey, embarrassed, could regain her footing. The experience taught her to be aware at all times while she worked, even if it seemed to be a trivial situation.

At the Silverdome parking lot, crowds of people, young and old, sang and yelled along with the band, in spite of not being able to see the performance. The smell of marijuana wafted through the air, and cans of beer could be seen in most of the revelers' hands. There were no fights, no vandalism at the moment, and nothing for them to do but keep an eye out for trouble and enjoy the music and the summer night.

I wonder if Brad would like to attend a concert here? I prefer Pine Knob with its outdoor theater and lawn seating, but this could be fun, too.

Lost in thought, she didn't notice Scott Fuller, her partner for the night, approach her. The other two officers on the scene were handling disturbances farther away.

"Hey, Stanton, are you going to stand there daydreaming or help break up the fight starting over there?" He pointed to a group of young men who were yelling at each other and occasionally throwing wild punches that didn't connect. They were clearly drunk.

"Let's go see what's going on." Aubrey unconsciously set her facial expression into a more menacing version of herself. Eyes slightly narrowed, mouth set and shoulders back, she added a slight swagger and walked off to the group, a step ahead of Fuller. She knew she couldn't afford to be too friendly, or they might overpower her. *The last thing I need is to look incompetent in front of Fuller.*

Before she could attempt a diplomatic approach, Fuller converged on the group, shouting, "Police! Knock it off." He grabbed one of the men and pushed him to the side, attempting to separate the parties.

Aubrey grabbed another one and put the flat of her left hand against his chest. The man sneered at her and tried to yank her hand off him. Putting to use a technique she'd learned in the academy, she reached over with her right hand, seized his pinkie finger, and bent it back toward his wrist. When he refused to let go, she bent it until she felt it break. He screamed and dropped his hold.

Aubrey handcuffed her troublemaker. "Sit down and don't move."

While she was handling the one man, Fuller wrestled on the ground with his opponent but was not winning. She stepped over to help him. Aubrey feared she couldn't physically overpower the burly drunk, so she pulled her baton and smacked his right forearm. He fell to the ground howling.

Fuller stood up, scowled at Aubrey, and handcuffed his target. They walked the men to their patrol cars, frisked each of them, and secured their detainees in the rear seats. They called for an ambulance to check out the injuries. There were a few more similar confrontations before the night was done. Several people were detained, and others let off with a warning.

****

Back at their own station, Scott's glare showed how angry he was about the help Aubrey'd provided in arresting his brawler. She'd changed into jeans and was walking out of the restroom when she caught his eye. He glowered at her.

She turned her head and continued to her car, knowing his anger would escalate if she gave him the chance to confront her. She drove home, listening to the radio, and singing along, washing away the traces of his hostility.

****

Anger consumed Scott as he sat in his patrol car. *Now that bitch showed me up at the Silverdome. Did she really think I couldn't handle that guy? How dare she interfere with my arrest? Women shouldn't be in protective roles. I learned that when I was six years old and my mother let my baby brother drown in the bathtub. I knew then women couldn't be trusted to take care of others, in spite of how society thinks of them as caregivers. Stanton needs to go ... and soon.* He pounded the steering wheel, then glanced around the lot, hoping no one was watching him.

****

When Aubrey entered her house, she saw the light blink on the answering machine, showing two messages. After greeting Kizzy, she pushed the button to listen to her first message.

"Hey, Bree, it's Brad." *Bree?* "I wanted to tell you again how much I enjoyed dinner the other night. I was also wondering if you would you like to go to a Bonnie Raitt concert next Saturday? It's at the Hill Auditorium in Ann Arbor. Call me back when you get a chance."

I'm glad he called. I had a great time with him, too. Aubrey'd call him back tomorrow. She wasn't familiar with the musician he'd mentioned but looked forward to watching a live concert. She clicked the button on the machine for the next message.

A stranger's voice burst out of the machine, "What is your problem, bitch? Leave that old murder alone, or you'll regret it. You don't know what you're messing with, but keep asking questions, and you'll find out." The deep baritone timbre sent a shudder up her spine.

"How did they get my home number?" Aubrey said to Kizzy, momentarily taken aback by the threat. "I must be ruffling somebody's feathers. I'll take it as confirmation I was right to re-open this case. Hmmm, I'll have to be more aware of who's around."

Aubrey promptly double-checked all the windows and doors to make sure she'd locked them. Spencer was a small town, and it wasn't unusual for people to leave their houses unlocked, but she knew she couldn't take any chances. After pulling her drapes closed, she ate a dinner of mac and cheese and reviewed her notes on the evidence from the box.

I need to talk to Lori's folks. I'll ask about their side of things. Who knows? Maybe they'll say something I can use.

****

The next day, on Sunday afternoon, Aubrey went to see Mr. and Mrs. Harris. The old neighborhood hadn't changed since she'd lived there. Three bedroom, brick bungalows lined the street, mature trees towered over the manicured lawns. Pansies and marigolds bloomed from planters. She pulled in front of the Harris's home and took a deep breath.

I hope they'll be willing to talk to me. Aubrey's stomach clenched. *Maybe I should have called first. Well, I didn't. And like my dad always said, 'There's no time like the present.' Of course, he was usually referring to chores.*

She stepped out of her car, walked to the door, and knocked. Paint curled on the wood edge, dead bugs dotted the inside of the overhead light. *They're letting the house go. Lori's dad was always so good at maintaining everything. Does her death still affect him so much, he's neglecting things?*

Mr. Harris answered. Worn down by life and the murder of his only daughter, his shapeless brown cardigan hung on his bent and bony frame. Fringes of hair peeked out around his over-sized ears. *A specimen in a Petrie dish would get a friendlier look from him than I'm getting.*

"What do you want? We're not buying anything, and we're not listening to any speeches," he snarled at her.

I have to talk to them, regardless. "Hi, Mr. Harris. You may not remember me, I'm Aubrey Stanton. I was Lori's best friend."

"Hmph, some best friend you were. Why weren't you walking home with her the afternoon the killer snatched her?"

His words pained her, especially since she said the same thing to herself. "I'm sorry I wasn't with her. I relive those moments every day. I guess we'll never know if it would have changed anything." *I didn't expect his hostility toward me. I was a kid, myself. It's not fair to blame me for someone else's actions.*

"Likely excuse. I asked what you wanted here."

"Sir, I'd like to talk to you and Mrs. Harris, if it's okay. I'm a police officer now, and I'm looking into her murder again, hoping to find the one who did it."

"That other detective … Rollins was his name … he bothered us every day for weeks. He couldn't find out who did it. Why do you think *you* can?"

"I'm not certain —"

"Who's there, Ralph?" Mrs. Harris called from inside the house.

"It's one of Lori's old friends, Aubrey Stanton. Thinks now she's a cop, she can figure out who killed our little girl."

"Oh, for goodness sakes, Ralph, let her in."

"Not sure why I should, but, whatever, come in, *Officer* Stanton." He jerked his chin higher as he allowed her to enter.

"Thank you, sir," Aubrey said, avoiding his sarcasm and stepped into the living room. Aubrey was thankful Mrs. Harris didn't seem angry at her, also. Nothing had changed in fourteen years; the same furniture, the same layout, even the same smell of cooked cabbage permeated the air. The scene brought back intense memories.

I feel like I'm eight years old again. I used to love coming here to see Lori.

"Hello, Aubrey, dear. How nice of you to come by to see us," Mrs. Harris said as she hugged Aubrey, grounding her to the present. "I've missed you. What on earth brings you here today?"

"Hi, Mrs. Harris. I've missed coming here, too." She smiled at the woman. "I'm sorry to intrude. I was telling Mr. Harris I'm now a police officer, and I'm going over everything in Lori's case to see if there're any new leads to follow up on."

Lori's mother exemplified a 1950's mom. Her apron hung crisply over her blue dress, her faux pearls encircled her neck, makeup was perfect, and her auburn hair recently styled. She'd never worked outside the home. Instead, she spent her days serving her family's needs, as she had for more than thirty-five years.

"You look wonderful, Mrs. Harris. I hope things are going well for you."

"Yes, yes, everything's fine, Aubrey. Come in and have a seat and tell us what we can do to help."

Her husband muttered behind her as he closed the door. "Shouldn't she be helping us, not the other way around?"

"Yes, Mr. Harris, I *am* here to help you, but I need more information first. I'd like to ask you a few questions. Perhaps I can get closure for you, and put the person who did it in jail."

"Can I get you a cola or water to drink, dear?" Mrs. Harris was already heading toward the kitchen as she glanced back for Aubrey's answer.

"Water would be nice, thank you."

"Of course, one moment. Have a seat."

Mr. Harris sank onto their floral damask sofa. Aubrey sat in the matching, but too-soft armchair across from him. Mrs. Harris brought a glass of water to Aubrey, a beer for her husband, and sat next to him.

"Thank you." Aubrey took a deep breath and plunged in. "One of the questions I've always had was why Lori was walking through the park. Do you know? When we walked together, we never went there. We always took the sidewalk on the other side."

"We weren't convinced she *had* been walking through the park, until our older son, Jake, said he'd seen her there," Lori's mom replied.

"I vaguely remember your sons. They were quite a bit older than Lori, right?"

"Oh, yes, Jake is six years older, and Jamie is eight. When we were talking about it, Jake overheard the conversation and told us he'd seen her with someone. He thought the person was one of her friends and ignored them. He was anxious to get home and do his homework. He was always so studious, our Jake." A proud smile graced her lips.

"So, this other person was about Lori's age? Or size? I'm guessing you told Detective Rollins, correct?"

"We mentioned it to him, but he didn't seem to be interested in the details. I don't think he spoke to Jake about it, at least I'm not aware of the detective talking to him. Did he say anything to you, Ralph?"

"No, he didn't. I don't believe he had any idea how to find out who killed her, and I was right since he never did find him." His face contorted into an angry frown, as he crushed his beer can with his hand.

Aubrey turned toward his wife, keeping her face neutral in spite of the slight against the detective. "Mrs. Harris, did Jake say whether the person he saw was a boy or girl?"

"I don't think he could tell from the distance. I guess he assumed it was a girl." She clasped her hands, glanced upward as her words caught in her throat. Lori'd been gone for fourteen years, but the pain of her loss was still evident.

"Do you really think a friend could've killed her?" Mr. Harris's caustic words stinging.

Aubrey leveled her gaze at him. "I have no idea, but it would help if I could talk to Jake. Is he still in the area?"

Mrs. Harris, her emotions once again under control, said, "He moved to Mill's Creek a few years ago, so he's not very far. Should I tell him you want to speak with him?"

"Actually, if I could have his address, I'd rather he not know in advance I want to speak with him. People tend to get nervous when they know the police are looking for them. There's no reason he should be, but I also want spontaneous answers from him. If he thinks about his memory of this too much, it could change what he really saw and heard."

"I'll get his address for you. I'm sure he'll cooperate and tell you what he knows, but I'm not sure he knows anything." She got up and went to a table to write it down.

Mrs. Harris handed Jake's information to Aubrey. "It might be hard to catch him. He travels a lot these days. I wish he'd settle down around here so we could see him more often."

"I understand. Maybe one day, right? Thanks so much, Mr. and Mrs. Harris. If I think of anything else, may I call on you again?"

"Yes, Aubrey. We want to catch her killer. Please help us."

"I'll do my best. If you think of anything else, please call me. Here's my personal number." Aubrey handed her a card. *Not much to go on, but maybe I'll get something out of Jake.*

Chapter 7

Leaving the Harris's home, Aubrey mentally reviewed the bit of information she had. *Jake saw someone, approximately Lori's size or height, talking with her in the park. A place she wouldn't usually go after school. Did he, or she, lure her into the undeveloped area? Was she on her way somewhere besides home? But where?* Tapping her fingers on the steering wheel, she slowed down behind an elderly man driving at least ten miles under the limit, then turned on the next street.

How could someone the same age manage to kill her without Lori screaming for help? Would someone have even heard her if she had? I need to canvas the people on that side of the park next. I'll go on Saturday when more people will be at home.

Confident in her plan, she sped the rest of the way to her house.

Once she'd greeted Kizzy and grabbed a can of cola, Aubrey returned Brad's call from earlier.

"Hi, Brad. It's me, I got your message. I wanted to say I'd love to see Bonnie Ritter Saturday night with you."

Brad laughed. "It's Bonnie *Raitt*. I take it you don't know her, right?"

"Oh, gosh, sorry. No, I don't know her, but I've heard of her. I'd still like to hear her play. What kind of music is it?"

"She does a mean slide-guitar, blues-type music but also contemporary stuff. I think you'd like her. She's a strong, independent type, like you." His voice betrayed the smile she couldn't see.

Aubrey blushed at the compliment.

"Ahhh, yes, she does sound like my kind of woman. What time do I need to be ready?"

"I thought we could grab a bite to eat and head over to the concert. I'll pick you up at, say, five o'clock?"

"Sure, that's —" Commotion in the background at Brad's end interrupted her response, and she heard ferocious barking.

"Great, I gotta go. Talk to you later." He hung up.

Holding the handset, Aubrey looked at it as if it had answers to what had happened. "Oh, well, I'm sure I'll talk to him again before Saturday," she said with a sigh. "C'mon Kizzy, let's eat dinner."

After a meal of tacos and rice, she turned her radio to a soft rock station. She called Steve to ask about Jake's sighting of Lori in the park. She wanted as much information as possible before questioning Jake about it.

"Hi, Detect…Steve? Sorry, it's still a little weird calling you by your first name."

"Hi, Aubrey, it's okay. How's your case going?"

"Not as promising as I'd like, but I learned something I want to ask you about. I visited the Harrises, and Lori's mom told me her son, Jake, saw Lori in the park with a stranger. At least, he didn't recognize the person. Do you remember speaking to him? There's nothing in the book saying you did."

"Hmmm, I do vaguely remember her mentioning it, but at the time, we were following up on other leads. It must have slipped my mind. Wait, give me a second. I kept my personal notes about the case. Let me check."

Aubrey stood holding the phone, bopping her head and mouthing the words to "Hotel California" as it played in the background.

"Here we go. Sorry it took so long. I found a note about Mrs. Harris saying Jake saw Lori. I did talk to him, but he said he didn't know who it was. He said Lori was laughing, and they seemed friendly. There wasn't enough to follow up on. He couldn't even give a description except, whoever it was, was somewhat taller than Lori and wearing a blue coat."

"Oh, okay. Yeah, it's not much to go on, is it? I think I'll talk to Jake and see if he recalls anything else."

"I think it's a good idea, especially since you were close to his sister. He might offer you more information than he gave me."

"Maybe. I'll let you know. I'm glad I called you, though. At least I have a bit more to work with."

"No problem, Aubrey. Call any time. Goodnight."

"Goodnight, Steve," Aubrey said.

****

Tuesday morning, Aubrey had no idea the day would soon bring headaches and heartache. She was at the scene of a home invasion with a family of unreasonable and angry people. They had been shouting and talking over each other for an hour. She was on the verge of a migraine when dispatch contacted her with a 10-19 code, a request for her to return to the station as soon as possible. It took another thirty minutes to extricate herself from the warring couple.

After parking her car in the employee lot, she jogged across the gravel and hurried inside. Sergeant Mills waited in the hallway. His bulldog face appeared more solemn than usual.

"Hey, Sarge, what's going on?" she asked.

"Aubrey, please come into my office." He opened the door and gestured for her to go inside. "Have a seat."

"Okay ... you've never called me by my first name before, what's wrong?" She hadn't felt this nervous since her first week on duty. "What's going on? Am I in trouble? Sorry I haven't had a chance to bring you this week's report. I got a call—" His face betrayed concern and something she couldn't put her finger on. Her heart pounded in her ears. *Something bad's coming.*

Mills interrupted, "Your father was in a car accident."

"Is he all right? Where is he?" Aubrey prepared to bolt from the chair.

"No, he's not. The other driver was drunk and slammed head-on into your father's car." He swallowed and said, "Neither survived. I'm so sorry for your loss."

Aubrey struggled to stay calm, hands over her face. *Goddammit, get it together. I won't let him see me fall apart here. All these guys already think I'm too emotional.*

She stood up after a minute, eyes red but dry, took a deep breath, and asked, "Does my mother know yet?"

"Yes, she's been notified. She's waiting for you at her house."

"Thank you, sir." She clenched her teeth, blinked several times, held her mask in place.

"Aubrey, take as much time as you need. You have three days bereavement leave already, and I know you have some vacation time saved up as well. Let me know the arrangements, and when you're ready to come back to work. If there's anything I can do, please don't hesitate to ask."

"I will, thank you. I better go now." She straightened her spine, pulled her shoulders back, and settled a determined expression on her face.

"Aubrey, are you all right to drive? Do you want one of the other officers to take you?" His compassion touched her.

"I appreciate your concern, Sergeant, but Stantons don't let their emotions control them. My father always said hysterics and emotional outbursts aren't necessary … or helpful … and are not for public display." She fixed her gaze at him and added, "I have to go to my mom now."

Mills pressed his lips together and nodded at her. Aubrey retreated to the restroom, where she changed out of her uniform, feeling the knot in her stomach and her pulse racing as she continued to digest the information. She headed out to her car, encountering a couple officers who had already heard the news and extended their sympathies as she left the building.

Driving to her childhood home, her mind conjured the few memories she had of her father. *He was always working or yelling. Was his life so hard? I think he tried to do the best he knew for us, but it was never good enough for Mom. I remember when he bought her a car for Christmas; it was used, the wrong model, too old, not the right color. I could tell Dad was heartbroken after all his planning. I think he sold it and let her buy what she wanted. I was so sad for him.*

She wiped an errant tear from her cheek. She shook her head and her thoughts away. *Take it one step at a time, I guess.*

She turned onto the street where she'd spent her childhood. Since her parents' divorce, the lawn had become overgrown, the flowers were wilted or dead. The house had an empty feel to it these days. *Mom must be having trouble keeping up with the maintenance. Dad always took care of the house, and now he's gone*

. Aubrey parked in front of the house and saw her Mom's ice blue Lincoln Town Car in the driveway. *Maybe she should be using some of the money she paid for the car to keep the house up instead. Oh well, not my problem how she spends her money.* There was also a Crown Vic she didn't recognize. Jayne Stanton was currently dating a Lincoln-Mercury salesman, and she'd bragged to Aubrey about the new car he'd helped her buy. *The extra one must be his ... Paul, right?*

Aubrey collected her thoughts, walked to the door, and knocked. She rarely visited her mother and always felt like an intruder. Although it was the house she grew up in, she suspected she shouldn't simply open the door and walk inside. Her cop's *spider-sense* was on target as the door opened. Jayne's clothing looked disheveled, and her makeup was smeared. Her salesman was tucking in his shirttails.

Well, this is awkward. Don't roll your eyes, she admonished herself.

"Oh, Aubrey! I didn't expect you quite so soon. Come in, come in. You remember Paul, don't you?"

Paul managed a sheepish grin and a head nod, perched on the arm of the sofa, appearing ready to flee at any moment.

"Hi, Mom. Yes, I do. Hi, Paul. They called you about Dad, right?" Aubrey asked as her voice battled with sadness and scorn for her mother's impropriety.

"Yes, of course. I was your dad's emergency contact. It's terrible what happened. Someone driving drunk at his early hour of the day?" Jayne waved her hand as if swatting a fly. "Your brother's plane arrives this afternoon, and he wants to stay with you. Is that all right?"

"It's fine if he doesn't mind sleeping on the couch. I only have one bedroom. Do you want me to pick him up at the airport?" Aubrey was all business as she sat on the chair. *If I allow myself to react, I know I'll say something regrettable.* The new, modern furniture and lack of family photos were recent changes. *I guess Mom doesn't want to be reminded she's a mother these days.* An abstract painting of an orange and blue horse made Aubrey look twice. *Where on earth did that come from?*

"That would be wonderful, dear. I'm sure Tom'll be fine sleeping on your couch. He'll only be here a few days."

"You don't seem very upset about this. Did you hate Dad so much?" She squinted her eyes as she examined her mother's reaction.

Her mother had the good grace to pretend shock at Aubrey's question. "Why, of course, I'm upset. What a thing to say." Jayne wrung her hands as her eyes darted between her daughter and her boyfriend. "I don't see you bawling your eyes out over him, either."

"You and Dad trained me all my life to control my emotions. I'll grieve for him later, privately. Have you done anything yet about a service, or is there anyone I should call?"

"I'm waiting for Tom to get here, and I thought we could all sit down and discuss things. Maybe we can order in some dinner from *Faym-Us Chicken*. Would you like that? It was always your favorite."

"Fine. I don't know if I'll be hungry, but at least we can make some plans. What time do I pick up Tom?" Aubrey watched Paul trying to disappear into the couch. *I don't think he was prepared for this wonderful family reunion.*

"His plane is due in at two-thirty. He's flying United. I know he'll be glad to see you."

"Do you need me for anything? Otherwise, I'm going home to tidy up. I'll pick up Tom, and we'll come back here at five."

"Certainly. Go right ahead, and we'll see you in a few hours." Jayne gave her daughter a one-armed hug. Aubrey accepted it but didn't reciprocate.

"Okay. Bye. See you later." Aubrey struggled not to storm out of the house but managed to slowly and deliberately walk away, get into her car, and drive toward home.

****

Aubrey controlled her tears of anger and grief until she opened her front door and was greeted by Kizzy. The little dog sat patiently, sensing Aubrey's distress and waiting for a cue from her mistress. Aubrey sat on the floor, cuddled her friend, and cried.

He was only forty-nine years old. I can't believe it. Last time I saw him ... maybe three months ago, he was dating someone. I think her name was Wendy? Wilma? Juanita? Doesn't matter. Mom's not going to be happy if she shows up at the service, whoever she is. I don't know if they were still dating anyway. I wish things had been different for Dad and me.

When her sorrow abated, she got up, brushed herself off, let Kizzy outside, and washed her face. She retrieved fresh linens from the closet and set them on the end of the sofa, and placed clean towels in the bathroom. Aubrey took a look around. *I better dust. Tom's never seen my place. I don't want him to think I'm a slob.*

When everything was neat and orderly, it was time to leave for the airport. She hadn't seen Tom in nearly four years and anticipated a pleasant, if short, visit with him. *Not the best circumstances, though. I wonder how Tom'll react to being back here. He and Dad never got along, and the more Dad punished him, the worse Tom got. Maybe he'll be relieved Dad's gone. I guess I'll find out soon.*

Aubrey pulled up in the arrivals area where Tom waited. She honked her horn, and he sprinted to her car. She popped the trunk, so he could put his overnight bag inside. He climbed into the front passenger seat.

"Hey, Aubrey. Sweet ride," Tom said. "Reminds me of our old neighbor, Mrs. Tompkins's yellow Impala. Good to see you after so long. How ya doin'?"

"Thanks. I always liked her car and chose the Mustang because it was the same color, but sportier. I'm okay, Tom. I'm still dealing with the shock, though." She drew a breath. "I can't believe Dad's gone, can you?"

He scratched his head. "Yeah, it was a surprise, and work's not delighted I'm gone for a few days. I have a lot to do, and no one else can do it. They'll get over it."

"I have a few days off, too, but there are lots of people who do what I do, so it's not a problem. How was the flight?"

"It was fine. Mom said I'd be staying with you?"

Aubrey laughed. "Mom told me you *asked* if you could stay with me. I guess she doesn't want any guests other than Paul, her new boyfriend, at the house. I'm glad to have you, but I hope Mom explained I only have a couch to sleep on?"

"It figures she would manipulate the situation. I'd rather stay with you anyway, and a couch is fine with me. I've slept on worse. Of course, I'm hoping it's not a loveseat. Not sure my legs would like being cramped all night." Tom stretched his legs out as far as the car would allow for him to emphasize his point.

"No, it's full size. It's pretty comfortable, too."

"Cool. How's your investigation going?" He glanced sideways at her.

"I've found out a few things, but they aren't very helpful. I can't really talk about it. Do you remember Jake Harris?"

"I think so. He was older than me, so I never really knew him. Why?"

"I need to talk to him about Lori, and wondered if you had known him at all. I thought maybe you'd have some insight into who he is, what kind of guy. No big deal."

The siblings were quiet as the radio played softly in the background. They had never been close and always found small talk difficult. Aubrey felt awkward around her big brother, who was touted by their parents as being *so smart*, in spite of his mediocre grades and apathetic attitude. They excused those by claiming he was *bored* or *not applying himself*. It left Aubrey feeling unappreciated for *her* efforts and good grades.

"Mom wants us to come by for dinner and discuss the arrangements for Dad," Aubrey interrupted the silence and her recollections. "I'm sure Paul will be there as well. I don't really know him, but he strikes me as a typical sleazy car salesman."

"Sounds like Mom's ideal man." Tom chuckled. "She does love her new car."

"Here we are, home sweet home. C'mon in, and we can get caught up before dinner."

Kizzy scrutinized Tom as he entered the house. Even after Aubrey greeted her, she refused to go near him.

"Strange. Kizzy should remember you, and she's always friendly. Maybe it's the airplane smell on you. Oh, well, she'll warm up to you after a while. I have a home office you can put your stuff in if you'd like."

"Nice place you've got here." He smiled at his baby sister.

"Thanks. I'm not here very much, but I tried to make it homey. It works for me."

She showed Tom where he could set his bag and pointed out the rest of the house.

"I don't think you'll get lost in here, it's only about 800 square feet." Aubrey gestured toward the end of the hallway. "The bathroom is at the end of the hall. I put fresh towels for you on the shelf inside, and there are more in the linen closet. Let me know if there's anything else you need. Want something to drink?"

"Sure, if you've got a beer, I'll take one. If not, a cola is fine. Thanks."

After handing Tom his beer, she sifted through her brain to find something to talk about. She settled on, "By the way, did I tell you about my encounter with a humongous raccoon? Oh my God, scared the hell out me. Kizzy attacked it, and it bit her. She's okay now."

"Ha, a raccoon got the better of her? Where I live, we have bears, panthers, and elk to worry about. I think she'd be in trouble there."

For the next two hours, Aubrey and Tom laughed and talked about their childhoods. She carefully avoided any controversial subjects, like her investigation or her job.

She teased Tom about the time they'd gathered two dozen snakes: garters and blue racers, from Kensington Park. When they arrived home with their bounty, Tom put them in the bathtub while he hunted for his large aquarium. The snakes had a different plan and escaped, hiding throughout the house.

"Remember how we had to check our beds every night for unwanted guests? And how Mom screamed every time she saw one curled up in a closet, or wherever? I don't know if we'd ever have found them all without her shrieks!" said Aubrey, and they both laughed at the memory.

Tom's mouth quirked up in amusement. "Yeah, it was pretty funny, not to Mom or Dad, but still ... I remember when you fell in the deep end of the pool one winter evening. I couldn't figure out how you managed to get out of the water without the ladder. I can still see you standing on the back landing, dripping wet, in your heavy coat, boots, and mittens. How old were you? Ten? No one even knew you were outside." He glanced at her, eyebrow cocked. "Why *did* you go out? It was pitch dark, and we had two feet of snow."

When Aubrey didn't respond, Tom closed his eyes and shook his head. "Mom was so mad you wrecked their dinner party. Do you remember who was there?"

"No, but I remember feeling thankful I fell onto the ledge around the pool, or I might have drowned. How long do you think it would have taken them to realize I was gone?"

"Hmmm, probably only a day or two, at most."

Tom laughed, and after giving him the stink-eye, Aubrey joined in. She knew how close he was to the truth. But those hurts were long past. She'd accepted who her parents were, and had forgiven most of their shortcomings.

Tom went into the bathroom to freshen up after his flight. Aubrey took Kizzy for a short walk and to stretch her legs. At five o'clock, she raised her mental shield in preparation, and they drove to Jayne's house for dinner and

plan-making.

Chapter 8

Aubrey's mother ordered chicken dinners. As they ate, she, Tom, and Aubrey decided on arrangements for the funeral. Paul sat quietly off to the side, apparently enjoying his dinner.

"I think we should use Swanson's Funeral Home. It's nearby, and everyone is familiar with it. Besides," she glanced at him, "and excuse me, Paul, but I used to date George Swanson, and maybe he'll give us a deal. I broke up with him, and I'm sure he'll want to see me again. He was heartbroken afterward." She gently patted her perfectly coiffed hair, displaying her perfectly manicured nails. "And after all, it is the *best* and *most elegant* funeral home in town, you know," Jayne offered.

Tom snorted. "And because a *deal* is what we're *really* looking for, right, Mom?" Tom cocked his eyebrow. "I'm fine with Swanson's whether he gives us a discount or not."

"Mom, do you want to go with us to pick out the casket?" asked Aubrey, ignoring her brother.

"No, dear, you two can handle that detail. I'm sure you'll choose appropriately."

"Okay, do you know what the budget is? I'm assuming you know the value of his life insurance, but who are the beneficiaries? You, or us, or all three of us?" asked Aubrey.

"Aubrey, it's crass to speak about money," her mother chastised, glancing at Paul. "I'll need to speak with our attorney to find out if your father changed his insurance, or if he left a will."

"I'm only asking because we can't decide on anything without knowing how much it will cost and the amount we'll have to spend. I thought I was being practical. Sorry to be *crass*."

Tom chimed in, "Mom, why don't you call the attorney in the morning and find out the details. We can plan things from there, okay?"

"You're always so sensible about these things, Tom." Jayne patted his cheek, smiling smugly at Aubrey. "I'll take care of it tomorrow and let you know."

Aubrey clenched her teeth and resisted narrowing her eyes in irritation. *It's okay for Tom to talk about money, but when I do, it's inappropriate.*

The rest of the evening was challenging and uncomfortable. Everyone seemed to avoid verbal landmines, such as talking about their father, childhood memories, their jobs, and whether they would ever get married and have children. They managed to make inconsequential small talk about the Tigers' winning streak and the weather.

"Looks like Jack Morris and Lance Parrish make a good pair, don't they? Tom said.

Even Paul warmed up to the subject of baseball. "I went to college on an athletic scholarship for basketball. Yeah, I think this might be the year we win the Series. It's time."

Aubrey pondered Paul's comment. *I find it hard to believe this man with his paunchy belly and, at best, five-ten height played basketball. Maybe it depends where he went to college. I guess I don't really care enough to ask, though.*

"I'm tired," Tom said at eight o'clock. "Aubrey, let's go, and we'll call you tomorrow, Mom."

"Sounds good to me," Aubrey replied and practically leaped out of her chair. "Bye, Mom, Paul. Have a good night."

****

The next afternoon, Jayne called Aubrey. "Your father changed his beneficiaries to a fifty-fifty split between the two of you." She sniffed. "I'm surprised he left nothing for me. We *were* married for eighteen years, after all."

Aubrey listened to her mother's whining through the phone. His policy was large enough to cover the final expenses, give Aubrey and Tom each a tidy sum to supplement their income, and, once they sold his house, some extra to make their lives more comfortable.

The funeral arrangements were set for Thursday at ten a.m. None of them wanted to have visitation days or drag it out any longer than necessary. Since they weren't a close family, nobody complained about the speed of the proceedings. They ordered a brief obituary placed in the local paper, called a few relatives and known friends of their father. Tom agreed to do the eulogy. It was all settled.

****

The funeral home was beautifully decorated, yet somber. Soft choral music played in the background. The scent of lilies permeated the air, and Aubrey knew she'd never smell them again without thinking back to that day. The Spencer Police Department sent a beautiful combination of white roses, gladiolus, carnations, and Oriental lilies. The department and officers signed the card collectively and individually. It touched her that so many of them had participated. Several stopped by to offer their condolences. Those who weren't on duty stayed for the brief service.

Glancing around the room at the floral displays, one in particular, stood out. Aubrey walked over and took a closer look. The card was signed by a Teri F., who had sent an artful arrangement in a unique glass vase with blue hydrangeas, crème roses, blue delphiniums, and a delicate white flower she didn't recognize. *I think I'll keep those, they're pretty and smell so nice.*

Aubrey was surprised at the number of people whose lives her father had touched. She'd had no idea. They all spoke of him lovingly and said they'd miss him. Several times throughout the day, Tom and Aubrey exchanged incredulous glances across the spacious reception room. They didn't know the man these people knew. The person she remembered was humorless, strict, and indifferent. She wished she'd known this other person who they described as fun, silly, and smart.

Aubrey closed her eyes and recalled a scene she'd almost forgotten. *I was about ten years old and sitting on the floor of our kitchen, talking to Dad as he made fudge, the best fudge ever. He was laughing and singing, a rare event.* She smiled at the memory.

Opening her eyes, she found a woman standing in front of her. The woman wore a tremulous smile, and her head was cocked.

"Hello. You must be Aubrey?" She wore a black, knee-length, sheath dress that accentuated her slender figure, her light blue eyes appeared bloodshot. "I'm Teri. I was friends with John. I'm so sorry for your loss."

Ahh, the flowers I liked. "Hi, Teri. Thank you for the beautiful flowers. Nice to meet you. How did you know my dad?"

"We'd started dating a few weeks ago." A myriad of emotions flitted over her face. "We met at a Parents Without Partners Euchre tournament last month. He must not have mentioned me to you."

Aubrey pressed her lips together before answering. "Um, sorry, he didn't, but we didn't talk very often. So, being in Parents Without Partners, you must have kids, too?"

"Yes, I have a son. He's a police officer, like you. Scott Fuller? Do you know him?" She smiled brightly.

Aubrey was speechless. So many thoughts crowded her brain, she couldn't form words, and, for a moment, thought she might throw up. Her face paled, and her hands shook.

"Are you all right, dear?" Teri asked, sudden concern in her eyes. "Maybe you should sit down. I'm sure this whole business has been quite a shock. Your father was so young."

"Ah … ah … yes … I'm sorry, I'm not feeling well." Aubrey bolted from the room and ran to the restroom, where she collapsed onto a bench inside. *No, no, no, not Scott. Of all the people … Did Scott know my dad was his mother's new boyfriend? He better not show up here.*

She covered her face with her hands. *Oh, my God, his mom seems so kind, how could she possibly have raised such an ignorant, sexist jerk? Okay, okay, calm down, and go back out. Maybe she left.*

Aubrey took several deep breaths, splashed water on her face, and looking in the mirror, she adjusted her expression, so as not to give anything away. She crept back into the room and stood halfway between the door and the casket. Situated so she wouldn't have to look toward her dad's coffin, but close enough to connect with the mourners who approached her.

Tom saw her return, and from the other side of the room, gave her a quizzical look. She shrugged, hoping he'd understand. She didn't see Teri, and let go of the breath she'd been holding.

The funeral director can dispose of those pretty blue flowers, after all.

After the service ended. Aubrey said goodbye to the last of the visitors, spoke with George Swanson, accepted his condolences, and verified the final details of the burial. She thought about the differences between her memories of her dad, and those of the people who came to pay respects.

How much did Mom cause his constant foul mood? Or, was he unhappy being a father? I'll never know now, and I'd never ask Mom. It doesn't really matter anymore. He was who he was. I think everyone is different around different people. It's kinda sad how we all act differently to fit the situation.

The rest of the day went smoothly. The reception at a restaurant nearby turned into more of a wake than expected. Aubrey found herself laughing at stories about her dad and enjoying the presence of those who'd known John in a more positive light than she or Tom. The knowledge caused her to reconsider her beliefs and memories of him. She paid the restaurant bill and looked for her brother.

Time to go home. Where's Tom? There he is, in the hallway, flirting with some young, blonde girl. I can't tell who she is from here. Let's find out who's captured his attention.

****

Aubrey shoved open the front door of her house. Kizzy yelped and skittered out of her way.

As they entered, she turned on Tom. "I can't believe you were hitting on Erin. My God, Tom, she's barely out of high school," Aubrey snarled. "What were you thinking?"

"Hey, she's a babe, and I thought, 'Why not?'" he replied.

"Because you're only here for a few days. What if she has a crush on you and you leave? Are you ready for a long-distance relationship?"

"Oh, for cryin' out loud, Aubrey. It was a bit of fun. Have you forgotten what fun is? Has your life turned into a daily melodrama without any comic relief? Lighten up."

"No, I have fun. In fact, I'm going to a concert tomorrow night with a guy I've started seeing. I know how to have a good time. My job is serious. How I act in public reflects on the department, and police in general."

"Really? What a load of self-righteous crap. You're only twenty-two. You should be out partying instead of working on old, musty, cold case murders. I'll bet you're a blast at the bar, interrogating everyone about how much they've had to drink. Borrriiinng." He flopped on the couch and crossed his arms, glared at her.

"Why should you care how I spend my time?" Fury staccatoed her words. "Lori was my best friend, and her killer's never been found. She deserves to have someone still hunting for whoever did it. Besides, I heard you mutter about this case opening old wounds after I spoke to you about the glass fragments."

His eyes widened in surprise, and his next words sounded contrite. "You weren't meant to hear me. I don't want to see you hurt by bringing it up again."

"What do you know about her murder, Tom? You're four years older than me. Do you know who the stranger was in the park with her? Did any of your friends ever talk about it, hint about possibly knowing who did it?" She stood in the kitchen doorway, braced against the frame, eyes narrowed, and mouth pursed as she waited for his answer.

He jumped up from the couch. "Why would you ask me such a thing? How dare you! Don't you think I would have said something to the detective who kept nosing around the house, saying he still had questions for you? I think you liked being the center of attention for a change." Anger rose along with his voice.

"You haven't matured a bit, have you? Maybe if you lived in a place with more than old, crusty miners in it, you'd understand. I lost a lot of friends after she died, and the other kids treated me like I was somehow tainted by simply finding her. Some thought, and said, *I* did it. You have no idea how awful school was for me. Certainly not the kind of attention anyone wants."

Aubrey slammed her hand on the coffee table, walked into the kitchen, and let Kizzy out the back door. She returned and berated Tom again.

"Were you jealous you *weren't* the major focus for once? Smarty-pants Tom, being left out of the action. Poor baby," Aubrey taunted her brother.

"Whatever. I'm going out. I'll call a cab." He stood. "Don't wait up for me, but I'll need a key. I'm going home tomorrow. I'd appreciate a ride to the airport, but if you don't want to take me, I'll call a taxi."

"You can take my car. I'm not going anywhere tonight. Of course, I'll take you to the airport tomorrow." She drew a deep breath, hesitated, looked at the floor, and added, "I'm sorry. We sound like children. I don't want to argue with you." Aubrey chuckled. "Almost like old times, isn't it?"

Tom shot a wry grin at her. "Almost. See you in the morning."

"Stay out of trouble, Tom."

Chapter 9

The next morning, Aubrey dropped Tom at the airport. She could tell he was feigning sleep on the short drive. She regretted the argument they'd had, but there was nothing she could do about it now. She needed to get to Lori's brother's house. There was no point sitting around her house, moping while she was off work. Might as well keep working on the case.

Jake lived in an older section of Spencer in what was known as a shotgun house. Shotgun houses comprised most of the streets. The style was a narrow rectangular home, approximately twelve feet wide, with rooms arranged one behind the other, and doors at the front and back. The name refers to being able to shoot a shotgun from the front door and have the bullet go right through the house and out the back. The houses sat a minimum distance from each other, leaving little space for lawn or plantings.

Aubrey rang the doorbell several times, but Jake wasn't home or wasn't answering. She glanced through the front window, but the drapes were pulled tightly closed. Aubrey looked around and saw his mailbox contained a few letters. She pulled one out to verify she was at the correct address and put it back in the box. Then she walked to her car, disappointed he wasn't home.

Darn it, I wanted to talk to Jake as soon as I could to avoid his mother telling him about our conversation, but Dad's funeral delayed everything. Aubrey mentally crossed her fingers, hoping Mrs. Harris hadn't blabbed to him. She would try again later.

With nothing else to do at the moment, she took Kizzy to the park. It was a beautiful spring day, and it had been several weeks since they'd been anywhere together. Aubrey let Kizzy run around the playground, climbing the slide, and scooting back down was one of her favorite activities. She was sitting on a bench watching her dog sniff the ground when a gigantic, black Rottweiler bounded out of the trees toward them. She jumped up, ready to grab Kizzy out of its reach, when she heard a familiar voice shouting, "Bubba! Bubba! Get over here, now!"

As Brad approached, he recognized Aubrey. His face broke out in a huge smile. "Hey, what are you doing here on a Friday? Not working today?" He said to his dog. "Bubba, sit."

"Hi, Brad. No, I have the day off. My father's funeral was yesterday. I'm going back to work on Monday. How are you?"

"Oh, man, I'm sorry. I didn't know. Had your dad been sick?" His voice quieted, revealing his sympathy. He gave her a quick hug, then waited for her to explain.

"No, it was a car accident. We weren't close. I'm all right. Are we still on for tomorrow?"

"Of course, if you feel like going? I'm sorry I hung up so fast the other night. Bubba knocked over my aquarium. You can imagine … water and fish everywhere, the carpet was soaked, Bubba was trying to catch the fish … it was chaos." He laughed.

Aubrey laughed with him, visualizing the scene. "I wish I'd been there. I'll bet it was pretty funny. Not at the time for you, though. Did you save the fish?"

Brad grinned. "All but one." He glared at his dog, who lowered his head as if embarrassed. "Bubba thought it looked like a snack."

He turned toward Aubrey. "I really am sorry. I was going to call you back the next day, but things got a little crazy. I'm glad I ran into you now. Where would you like to go for dinner tomorrow? There are some great little restaurants in Ann Arbor."

"I don't really know the town very well, so you pick someplace."

"Okay. I know, let's go to the Monkey Bar, great food and atmosphere. I'll pick you up at five?" Aubrey nodded. "I've gotta get going. See you tomorrow." Brad and Bubba raced back across the park as Aubrey waved.

I wish I knew what was going on with him. Our conversations always end so abruptly.

Kizzy lay on the ground, panting. "C'mon, girl, let's go home. You look tired." Aubrey ruffled the dog's fur, and they walked back to her car.

***

Aubrey scooped up the linens and towels that Tom had used, threw them in the washer, grateful her rental house had a washer and dryer, so she didn't have to use a coin laundry. She ate dinner and left to go back to Jake's place. On the way to his house, after months of perfect, balmy spring weather, the sky had turned dark; the heavy, rain-laden clouds, swollen to the point of bursting. *Looks like we're in for a good, old-fashioned thunderstorm. No thunder or lightning yet.*

She pulled in front of the house. A late-model, black Camaro sat in the driveway. She walked to the door and knocked, heard someone yell, "Just a minute," and waited. The door opened a few inches, and a man looked out through the gap.

"Hi, can I help you?" he asked.

"Are you Jake Harris?"

"Yeah, who are you?" Wary, but not unfriendly.

"Mr. Harris, my name is Aubrey Stanton. I was a good friend of Lori's. Do you remember me?"

"Aubrey? Sure, Lori talked about you all the time, but I don't remember ever meeting you." He opened the door wider.

"Do you mind if I come in? I have a few questions about the day she disappeared."

"Certainly. I'm sorry. Come in. I don't get many guests. The ... the place is a mess," he stammered, and he waved her inside, but turned his face away, hiding his obvious embarrassment. "Here, let me move those papers so you can sit." He grabbed the armload of papers and moved them to the kitchen table.

She'd had no idea how gorgeous Jake was. Medium-length, dirty blonde hair casually fell over his forehead, nearly obscuring his intense, deep blue eyes. The scar on his cheek enhanced his rugged features, and his toned, athletic body moved as graceful as a panther. His expression had shifted. His eyes had been narrowed, and his mouth compressed, but now his eyes opened, and his lips changed into a cautious smile.

Aubrey surveyed the living room. It was cluttered with stacks of books, papers everywhere, and discarded clothing. Two dark leather armchairs and one table sat positioned on the bright, multi-colored rug. A duffel bag, overflowing with clothing, and an enormous backpack with camera equipment spilling over the top sat in a corner. The lack of furniture was more than made up for with the abundance of unframed photographs pinned on the walls.

If Jake was the photographer, he was an exceptionally skilled one. Looking at them, Aubrey imagined strange and exotic, wild places. The eerie lighting and compositions were powerful. The shots with people were occasionally blurred, but expressive. She was no expert but could tell these were works of art, not amateur picture-taking. Mesmerized, she found it difficult to tear her eyes away.

Jake observed her reactions to his work. "What do you think? Do you like 'em?" he asked.

"They're beautiful ... and captivating. These are yours?" He smiled at Aubrey's compliment and nodded. "I didn't know you were a photographer. Is this a career or a hobby?"

"Thanks. It's a career. I work for *National Geographic*. You're lucky you caught me at home since I'm usually on the road. Sorry the place is such a mess. I don't have time when I'm here to worry about cleaning it."

Aubrey watched him, looking for signs of nervousness or deception, but found none. She smelled a cacophony of smells: the warm, pungent aroma of coffee and the greasy pepperoni pizza on the counter, overlaid with a gamey, sweaty odor of unwashed clothes. But when he stood behind her, the only fragrance she inhaled was his spicy and earthy cologne. Aubrey closed her eyes, then shook her head to clear the illicit thoughts she had. *Focus Stanton, quit thinking about him as anything other than a witness.*

"It sounds fascinating, Jake. Is it okay if I call you Jake?" She waited for him to sit on the other chair before seating herself where he'd indicated.

"Yeah, it's fine. I enjoy it, but not the traveling so much. It gets old after a while. I'm only here for one more day, and I'm off to Morocco. As for that day in the park, I'm not sure what I can tell you, Aubrey, or why you're asking."

"I'm sorry, I forgot to mention I'm a police officer in Spencer now. I'm unofficially reviewing her case, which is why I'm not in uniform."

"Do you have news about who killed her?"

"No, not yet. I spoke to your parents several days ago. Your mom mentioned to me you'd seen Lori on the Monday she went missing. She said you'd seen someone with her. Do you recall any more?"

Jake shrugged. "I told the cops at the time about it, but they never came back to ask more questions about it."

"Can you tell me what you saw? If you close your eyes and think back, it might bring the memory into a better view." She tilted her head and raised her eyebrows in question.

He shook his head. "I don't need to. I think about it every day, and how if I'd only walked over to her, I might have saved her from that creep. My dad still hasn't forgiven me. He told me I was responsible for her, being older, and I let her down, let them all down. I don't blame him, I haven't forgiven myself." He stood and paced around the room, hit the wall with the side of his fist, hung his head.

"Jake, it's not your fault. I felt the same way too. If I hadn't sent her on ahead of me, if I'd turned down the teacher's request for help, if, if, if. It gets you nowhere. The only person responsible is the one who killed her. I'm hoping your sighting of the stranger she was with, will help me find her killer and bring this to a close, for all of us." Aubrey clasped her hands together and leaned forward as she watched him.

Outside, lightning exploded like gunshot and flashed across the room, as an earth-shaking clap of thunder boomed overhead. An avalanche of rain struck the roof. They both startled, and Jake walked over and looked out the window.

"Wow, we're in for a good drenching. It's been so dry, we can use it." Jake took a deep breath, ran his hands through his hair, and returned to his chair.

"You're right. I haven't talked about this for so long, and my parents wouldn't tell me anything. I'm glad you're looking into it again. Thanks."

He raised his eyebrows in a hopeful look and continued, "I told the detective I saw a person wearing a blue coat, standing with Lori in the wooded part over by Garrison Street, the east side of the park. He was maybe a foot taller than Lori, and they were laughing."

"You could hear the laughing, but not the conversation?"

"Right. I was too far away. I wondered at the time why she was in the park at all. She didn't usually walk there. It made no sense, but I thought she'd met a friend, so I continued on home. I had a big science project to finish."

"Jake, if you close your eyes and bring back the memory of them laughing, do you recognize the other person's laugh? Think about it. It had to be someone *she* knew, so *you* may have known the mystery person, also. Can you try … please?" She bit her lower lip, willing him to agree.

He sighed. "All right, I'll try." He shut his eyes and concentrated. The storm crackled and pulsed, streaks of light blazed as the thunder rumbled, and rain drummed on the house.

Jake's eyes popped open. Lightning illuminated Aubrey's face in an uncanny profile.

With a shock of recognition, he stared at Aubrey. "Oh, my God, I think it was your brother."

Chapter 10

"What? My brother? You mean Tom, right?" Aubrey exclaimed in disbelief. "Jake, I didn't realize you knew him well enough to know his laugh. I didn't think you knew him at all."

"Sure, I knew him. We were both in the Science and Chess Clubs at school. I knew him pretty well, in fact. We didn't hang out together, but we spent a lot of time at the meetings and playing chess. He was an outstanding player, and he beat me nine out of ten times." He grinned. "I'm not any better now, he'd probably win all ten games."

Tom told me he didn't know Jake. Why did he lie about it? Aubrey was confused and not sure where to go with this information, or what questions to ask.

"Um ... okay ... I'm a little blown away, as I'm sure you can tell. Could you write a statement about what you remember, and sign and date it for me? I'll need to put it in the file, and since you're leaving town, it'd be better if I got it from you now before you go."

"Yeah, I guess so. I can't believe Tom would have hurt her, though." Jake furrowed his brow and shook his head, got up, and walked around his living room, avoiding the piles of books on the floor. "It doesn't make sense. I don't know why I didn't figure this out a long time ago. It may have been the lightning strike that allowed me to see the similarity between *your* profile and your brother's."

"Possibly, your mind didn't want to accept it at the time. It wasn't important to you until later, and by then, you were dealing with shock and grief. I agree. I can't imagine Tom hurting her. I'll have to talk to him and find out more. But this is information I didn't have, so it moves us one step closer to discovering who did hurt her."

"It makes sense, I guess. Let me write it down for you, but I have to clean up and go see my parents. I'm leaving in the morning, and I try to spend time with them when I'm home. My older brother, Jaime, lives in Oregon in some commune, so he hardly ever comes back here." He sniffed the air, grimaced. "I have to do some laundry, too."

He sat at the table and scribbled a statement for her. After signing and dating it, he handed the paper to her.

"Jake, I have to ask you not to tell your parents yet, okay? I need time to work on this, and I'd hate for them to get upset if it turns out to be nothing."

He stared at the floor for a minute, lips pressed together, and finally agreed. "Okay. I'll keep this to myself for now. Let me give you my work number, and if you do find anything out, please call and leave a message. I'll get back to you as soon as I can. Agreed?"

"Yes, of course. Let me give you my personal number, and if you think of anything else, please call and leave a message, as well." Aubrey wrote her number on a piece of paper she found on the table. "I'll get out of here so you can do what you need to do. Thanks for your help, Jake. I appreciate your time." She stood and moved toward the door. "Have a safe trip."

"Thanks, Aubrey. It was nice meeting you, even if it was about a sad subject." He offered his hand to shake but drew back before she made contact. "Oh, wait a minute. It's not as good as the ones out here, but I have a photo of Lori I'd like to give you. I was always taking pictures of everyone, as far back as I can remember."

He left the room, returning moments later with a haunting photo of her friend.

"Wow, it's ... stunning!" Aubrey clasped the picture over her heart. "Thank you so much. I'll treasure this. It's a remarkable gift."

Jake handed her a folder from a stack of papers. "Here, you can use this to keep it dry."

She carefully inserted the photo and held it against her chest.

The thunderstorm had abated while they'd talked, but drizzling rain lingered. Jake opened the door for her, and she jogged to her car, trying to outrun the falling drops. Her thoughts tumbled over the possibilities and emotions the visit created.

****

Saturday morning, Aubrey woke at first light. Her dreams had transported her to her childhood and back again, living and reliving details both true and false. As with most sleep-lives, they dissipated into vapor when her eyes opened.

"Good morning, Kizzy. I hope you slept better than I did." She stretched and yawned. "C'mon, I'll let you outside and get your breakfast ... mine, too. We have a big day today. I have to pick out something to wear on my date tonight, call Tom and find out why he lied to me."

After breakfast, she looked through her closet, pulled items of clothing out, inspected each one, and discarded it on the bed as unacceptable. Casual but 'date' pretty, she settled on a pistachio green silk blouse that brought out the color of her uncommon ice-green eyes. She chose boot-cut jeans, brown flats, and a simple gold necklace to complete her ensemble. She showered, read the newspaper, and had no excuse for not calling her brother any longer.

"Hi, Tom. How was your flight?" Aubrey asked.

"Hey, kid. It was fine, thanks. Everything all right?"

"Well, not exactly." *There was no point pussy-footing around.* "I met with Jake Harris last night, and he told me he knew you, knew you fairly well, in fact. Why did you lie to me?"

Tom sighed, and Aubrey waited.

"I guess I didn't see what good it would do to tell you. I thought it would cause trouble for me, and I don't need that. Yes, I knew Jake."

"He claims he saw you in the park with Lori the day she disappeared. You know it implicates you in her death, right? Is that the trouble you were trying to avoid? Because that's a problem. Tell me what happened." Her frustration mounted, and she paced back and forth as far as the phone cord would allow.

"Okay, yes, I did see her walking alone and approached her. She told me you'd stayed late at school to help the teacher with something. Lori was looking for pretty leaves for some project or something. She told me she didn't normally walk through that section of the park. We talked for a few minutes, then I left her and went home. I never gave it any thought."

"So, let me get this straight. You left her in the park, alone, and didn't think to mention it to the police after I told you I found her dead a few days later? Never once thought to say anything?" Aubrey felt her pulse race, and her frustration turn to anger.

"No, I didn't. There was no one else there, and nothing for me to say since I didn't know anything," Tom growled into the phone. "Are you accusing me?"

"I'm not, but it looks pretty suspect to me. You chat with her, and a few short hours later, she's reported missing? Someone else was there or close by. Are you sure you didn't see anything or anyone?"

"I'm sure. If that's all you wanted, I have to go. I have things to do." Tom hung up with a bang.

Aubrey slammed her phone down. *Now what?*

****

After scrubbing the floors furiously, and polishing the tables until they shone, it was time to get ready for her date. She took a shower and curled her hair, something she rarely bothered to do. Her shoulder-length, chestnut-colored hair had a natural wave and held curls easily, sometimes too easily, particularly in humid weather. Those times, she fought with the frizzies all day. Satisfied with her hair and a touch of makeup, she dressed.

Hmm, five minutes to wait. Let Kizzy out? Yes, good idea.

"Kizzy, go outside and do your business. Brad'll be here soon."

She opened the back door and watched Kizzy hesitate, then jump over thick, almost maroon, liquid on the back steps.

"Is that blood?" She knelt to get a closer look and smelled the distinct coppery tang. Her stomach heaved in revulsion. "Yes, it is. That's disgusting, who would do that?" *I'll bet it's my phone harasser. This idiot is getting too close. I need to keep Kizzy safe inside.* "Hurry, Kizzy," she yelled.

Her phone rang, and she turned back into the house to answer it, thinking it would be Brad.

"Hello?"

"Hey, bitch, did you get my message? I left you a present on the back door." She recognized the baritone, threatening voice from the previous message on her answering machine.

"Who is this?" she demanded, but a dial tone greeted her. *What a jerk.* She hung up and ran back to the porch, went outside, and found a dead possum duct-taped to her door. She looked around the yard and called Kizzy again.

"Here, girl, come." Aubrey and Kizzy stepped inside, and she locked the doggy door. The doorbell rang. "Great. Now Brad's here, and I have this mess to deal with." She opened the door for Brad and waved him into the house.

"Hi, Brad. I have a problem that's going to delay our date. I'm sorry."

She told him the story of the message from last week and what she'd discovered on the porch, as well as the phone call she'd received a few minutes ago.

"That's terrible, Bree. Is it someone you might know? I can help you clean it up."

His nickname for her made her smile. She'd never had one before except for 'Squirt' that Tom called her when she was younger. "I'd love that, but I need to call the station and report it. The possum and blood need to stay there until they finish dusting for prints, and they'll probably take the poor dead thing to see if there's any evidence on it. I don't think we're going to make it to dinner."

"We can go to dinner another time, but I'd like the coward who did this caught. Do you think it has anything to do with your case?"

"Yeah, I'm sure it does. Let me call it in, and maybe we'll still have time to see the show."

****

The crime scene techs retrieved, bagged, and signed for the evidence on the possum: scraped, dabbed, and photographed the blood on the door and porch. Aubrey wrote out a statement regarding both phone calls she'd received, and ninety minutes later, she and Brad were on their way to the concert.

"I think we have time to stop for a bite if you'd like. There'll be an opening act with Sippie Wallace, and it doesn't matter if we don't see her. She's good, but I'm okay with missing it. Bonnie doesn't start until eight o'clock. What do you think?" Brad asked.

"Okay, that sounds good. I *am* hungry. I'm sorry it took so long for the techs to finish."

"I actually thought it was fascinating, so I didn't mind at all. I hope they figure out who it is. You never mentioned you'd received a previous call from the creep."

"We haven't had much chance to talk since it happened. Random calls, threats, all kinds of people like to vent in anonymous messages to the police, but it was the first one I'd gotten at home. Can we forget it for the night and enjoy ourselves? I've had enough drama lately."

"Absolutely. I'm looking forward to watching Bonnie play, and I hope you enjoy her show."

They went to the Monkey Bar regardless of the short timeframe available. The small restaurant was actually a neighborhood bar, with the requisite dartboard, dim lights, jukebox, and a well-used, full-length, coffee-colored bar and Naugahyde-topped stools. A dozen tables scattered about with no rhyme or reason, managed to produce a cozy, casual atmosphere. Neon signs decorated the walls. In spite of its shabby appearance, the bar was busy and smelled marvelous. Aubrey's mouth watered.

As they ate hamburgers and fries, Aubrey asked, "Can you tell me more about the concert we're going to?"

"Sure. Sippie Wallace will most likely be done when we get there, but her music is blues and jazz, more like Bessie

Smith, and she also worked with Louis Armstrong, once in a while.

He sang off-key, *"When I woke up this morning, Had the up the country blues, When I looked over in the corner, My grandma had 'em too."*

He laughed along with Aubrey. Brad's face reddened as other patrons joined in the laughter, clapping at his performance, but he stood and took a quick bow.

"That was pretty bad, Brad. I hope Bonnie sings better than that."

His eyes lit up as he spoke. "Bonnie's amazing."

Teasing and laughing, they finished their meal, paid, and left for the auditorium.

****

As they drove toward the venue, Brad told her a little about its history. "The Hill Auditorium opened in 1913 and has magnificent acoustics. It's considered one of the world's great concert halls and has hosted a lot of different orchestras, speakers and music concerts. I love seeing shows here.

"We missed seeing Harry Chapin last month. Frank Zappa and Billy Joel are scheduled this fall. Would you like to see either of them?" Brad asked. "Or, if you prefer jazz, The Preservation Hall Jazz Band is performing in October."

Aubrey was amused at his excitement and willingness to please. It was a nice change from her last boyfriend, who only cared about race cars and boxing, her interests ignored.

She placed her hand on his arm for a moment and grinned. "Let's see how things go, but I'd be happy to see any of them with you, Brad."

They took their seats in the center of the mezzanine and waited for Bonnie to appear.

When the concert was over, they stopped for coffee at a small diner and reviewed the show.

"So, what did you think?" Brad asked Aubrey.

"It was fun. I enjoyed it, and I thought Bonnie was fantastic. What was that one song that the audience seemed so familiar with?"

"Oh, I think you're talking about her new song, Runaway. It's on her album *Sweet Forgiveness*. She played several from it tonight. I'm glad you enjoyed it."

"I've never seen anything like it. Thanks for inviting me." She gave him a huge smile and felt a red flush creep up her neck.

Brad bit the side of his lip, and Aubrey wondered what he was mulling over.

"I know things have been a little 'jerky' since the school presentation," he began. "Not the way I would normally start dating someone. I mean, usually, I would call more often, hoping for a long-winded conversation, while trying to decipher everything about you." He chuckled. "But between your work and your dad and my stuff, I haven't had the time to spend with you. I'd like to see you again. What do you think?"

He looks like a little boy asking for a cookie. He's so sweet. How can I say no to him?

"Yes, Brad, I'd like that." She smiled. "But it's late now, and I need to go home. It's been a long week."

"Okay, let's go." His broad smile crinkled the corners of his eyes, his face radiant.

The drive home was uneventful. They talked about music and art, arriving at Aubrey's house only minutes before midnight.

Brad walked Aubrey to her door. She unlocked it and turned toward him with hopeful eyes. He leaned forward and covered her mouth with his, in a hungry kiss. She closed her eyes as her heart raced, and she responded eagerly to his warm mouth and soft lips, tasting wintergreen on his tongue. The smell of night jasmine filled the air.

Aubrey lost herself in the kiss until Kizzy's barking inside the house interrupted them.

She laughed as they broke apart. "I think Kizzy has missed me. Thanks again, Brad. I enjoyed myself and would like to see you again. Good night."

"Good night, Bree." He turned and walked to his car. Aubrey heard him humming softly.

She entered the house, closed and locked the door, leaned back against it, touching her fingers to her lips. *He's an excellent kisser. I'd like more of that.*

"Hi, Kizzy. I had the most fabulous time tonight. Let's get ready for bed."

****

Aubrey woke late Sunday morning. She scrambled some eggs, toasted two pieces of bread, and poured a large glass of orange juice. She picked up the paper from her front door stoop, sat down at her kitchen table to enjoy her breakfast, and read the news.

The headlines shouted **Woman found dead in park.** *Oh, my god, no, no, no.* Her stomach curdled, and she pushed her plate away. "I can't eat now." She scanned the article for information but found little to nothing revealed. Aubrey hadn't expected anything, but hoped they'd say something important.

Aubrey dropped the paper on the table and sat back, covering her face. *Is this my fault? Did I antagonize the killer and re-ignite his desire to murder? Is it connected to the phone calls I've gotten? Is this what the caller meant by 'I'd regret it?' This is horrible, and all my fault.*

She slammed her hand on the table. "No. It isn't my fault," she declared. Her sudden anger startled the dog, who looked at her and whimpered. "It's okay, Kizzy. I'm furious with myself for thinking, for even one minute, that I have anything to do with a madman's behavior." She patted the dog's head, and Kizzy settled again under the table.

"Now, I *must* find this person, whoever it is, even if it's someone I know."

Chapter 11

Monday morning roll call covered the new murder in the park. Sergeant Mills emphasized that all officers should be aware of any suspicious behavior during their shift.

"I have a composite drawing from a witness who claims to have seen someone in the park late Saturday night. I'm not going to hand it out because it's so vague it could be anyone in the community, even one of us." His mouth twisted with scorn at the artist's lack of skill. "If we do our jobs, watch for anything out of the ordinary, and let the detectives do *their* jobs, we'll catch him. Now go protect and serve, and stay safe. Stanton, I need to see you in my office."

Everyone stood and started toward the door. Aubrey saw a couple of the guys glance her way and overheard them mutter, "Uh, oh."

She veered toward his office. Mills motioned her inside, shutting the door behind her.

"Hi, Sarge, I have the report you requested on the Harris case. I'd like to discuss a couple of leads I've come across."

"Aubrey, first things first. Are you sure you're ready to come back to work so soon? It hasn't even been a week." His face revealed nothing to her, simply scanned her eyes, and waited.

"Yes, sir, I am. My father and I weren't close. I'm fine, but thanks for asking. The flower arrangement from the department was beautiful. I don't know who sent it, but could you let them know it was appreciated, please?" She suspected it was Mills who'd organized it.

"Of course." He took a breath. "Okay, you can work, but if you find that it's too challenging to stay focused, tell me, and you can have the rest of the week off. Now, about those leads. The Harris file may no longer be a cold case if the detectives find enough similarity between it and the new murder. Detectives Brady and Weston are in charge of the new one. Go tell them about anything you've found out, and let them take over. You're off the case."

"But I...," she stammered.

"No buts, Stanton. You're done with it, for now, at least. If they don't find anything that leads to it looking like the same killer, we'll talk again. Go see them first, then get on patrol." Mills looked down, picked up papers, and Aubrey understood she was being dismissed.

She left his office and started toward the Detective's Bureau to share her findings. *If I tell them everything, they'll want to talk to Tom. Especially if they find out he was with Lori the day she disappeared. He was out by himself Thursday night, as well, when this new girl may have been killed. It does* not *look good for him.*

Aubrey ducked into the restroom to make a plan. She tore her report into tiny pieces, repeatedly flushing the toilet to make sure it was gone. *I'll go talk to them, but I'm not implicating Tom unless I find more evidence he was involved. I'm not giving up and handing this over to them, either. In all these years, no one else found out what I have.*

She found her way to the Detective's Bureau on the second floor. It was empty. *Well, that lets me off the hook ... for now.*

Aubrey sauntered out to her squad car to start her daily patrol. Everyone seemed to be in a hurry, so Aubrey wrote more speeding tickets in her one eight-hour shift than she had in the past three months. She was anxious about Tom's role in both murders. He'd never mentioned where he'd gone Thursday night. She recalled looking at her alarm clock upon hearing the front door open. It was after midnight.

I didn't notice him acting differently in the morning, but how would I know? I haven't seen him in so long, I don't have a clue how he usually acts, not anymore. And it's not like I do his laundry so I could check for bloodstains on his clothes.

She smacked her forehead. *What am I thinking? Could Tom have done these horrible things? No, not Tom.* On the other *hand, people are unpredictable, and anyone is capable of anything.* Aubrey shook her head in frustration and sighed.

Nearing the end of her shift, another officer requested back-up at a burglary complaint, so she put her ponderings on hold, responded to dispatch, and went to assist. It turned out the suspected burglar was the homeowner's nephew who'd forgotten his key. He'd been doing a poor job of attempting to enter the house through a window. The noise and fumbling in the blinds alerted his aunt, who called the police rather than checking it out herself.

"You did the right thing by calling for us to check," Aubrey assured the older woman, as her partner assisted the boy out of the window.

But when they questioned the young man, they saw his dilated eyes and lethargic movements. He was high, most likely on the preferred drug of choice, Quaaludes. She checked his pockets and found the pills and a small baggie of weed. They arrested him for possession and being under the influence of illegal drugs. By the time they booked him into the local jail, her shift was over.

Mark Jacobs, the other officer on the call, turned to Aubrey. "Would you like to go for a drink?"

Surprised at the invitation, she hesitated a moment, then said, "Sure, Mark." She hoped to finally be included as one of the team.

They met at The Pour House, the local cop bar whose owner, Gary Bailey, was a retired Spencer detective. They waved at the bartender as they entered and found a table by the wall. A server walked over, placed coasters in front of them, and asked, "What can I get you?"

"I'll take a Heineken with a glass of ice," said Aubrey.

"A glass of ice?" Mark questioned, raising his eyebrows. "A bottle of Miller's for me. Thanks."

To Aubrey, he said, "Heineken? Aren't you fancy?" He laughed.

"Oh, yeah, I'm a fancy beer drinker." Her acerbic tone appeared lost on her companion. "Sounds like an oxymoron to me, Mark."

"An oxy ... what?"

"Never mind." She shook her head. "That was an interesting collar today, wasn't it? If only the kid had remembered his key, he'd be home watching TV, or sleeping it off, instead of in jail."

"His aunt had no clue he was using 'ludes and weed."

The server returned with their drinks, setting them down on the cardboard coasters. Aubrey poured her beer over the ice in the glass provided. Mark raised an eyebrow but didn't comment. She didn't feel it was necessary to explain that the extra water kept her from being affected as swiftly by the alcohol. She always drank her beer that way.

"Poor kid. He needs help, really, not jail. So, what's up, Mark?" She took a long swallow from her glass.

"Nothing. I wanted to hang out with you. Have a beer, talk. Something wrong with that?"

"No, … but I've been in the department over a year, and this is the first time any of you guys have invited me for a drink, or anything, for that matter." She raised her eyebrows. "So, I figure something's up."

"Well, there's a first time for everything, right?" He gave a shrug and grinned at her across the table. "Honestly, I think you're cool, and although it was a little weird at first having a chick on the force, I think most of the guys have accepted it, by now. Except for Scott, of course. What's going on there?"

"I wish I knew. He's always had it out for me, so I try to avoid him as much as possible. I think he's arrogant and self-righteous, and probably hates women." Aubrey looked him in the eye, daring him to defend Fuller.

"He is kind of a jerk. You're right, but he's a good cop. I've worked with him a few times, and he's been great. He shouldn't harass you, though. We're all supposed to be on the same team, after all."

"Maybe someone should let him know that. Excuse me a minute, I need to use the restroom."

Aubrey got up, walked to the back of the bar, entered the women's restroom, and stared into the mirror. *I wonder what Mark really wants here. Seems a bit lame he would invite me for a beer, out of the blue like this. Maybe he hopes I know something about the murder.*

She glanced around the dingy bathroom, used the facilities, chuckled at the sign that read "Used Beer Depository," and washed her hands.

Perhaps, I can get him to talk about what the others are saying. They never share with me, and maybe, they know more than they're letting on. I like treasure hunts. Let's go see if I can dig up some gold nuggets.

As she returned to the table, she saw another bottle of Heineken at her place.

"Did you order this for me?" she asked Mark, her eyes squinted.

"Yeah. Your first one was all watered down, so I got you a fresh one."

"Thanks, where's my new glass of ice?"

"I didn't ask her for one. Why do you need it?"

She chose again, not to explain. "Because I like it that way." She raised her hand to catch the server's attention.

"So, Mark, what do you hear about this new murder? Do they have anyone on the radar for it?" Her glass was set down, and she poured her beer over the ice.

"Not much, it's too early. A couple of the guys overheard a detective saying it resembles the girl from the park twelve, thirteen years ago." He finished his beer and waved at the server for another one. "I didn't live here at that time, but I vaguely remember hearing about it. I was only a kid myself, so I didn't pay much attention."

So, he is learning things now, even without being involved in the investigation. I can be friendly… to a point.

"I *did* hear that you were somehow connected to the original dead girl, but couldn't figure out why you would've been. Weren't you a little kid, too?" Mark asked her.

"Yes, I was. It was actually fourteen years ago. Lori was my friend."

"Oh, wow. I'm sorry, I didn't know that."

"It's fine. It was a long time ago." She finished her beer. "Thanks for the beer, but I have to go. Maybe we can do this again?" *And maybe you'll have more information next time.*

"Sure, that'd be great. I think I'll stay and watch the game. See you tomorrow."

Aubrey waved at him and left the bar. Rain started to fall as she pulled into her driveway.

****

The next morning, Aubrey met with the detectives working the new murder case and shared that she'd interviewed

Lori's brother, Jake Harris. Hal Weston was thirty-ish, had chocolate brown hair, and a slim build. His affable personality made him the 'good cop' when they interviewed suspects. Rick Brady was in his early forties, surly, had thinning hair and a potbelly. He played the 'bad cop' and did it with a natural flair. She took an instant dislike to Brady.

    Aubrey told the detectives how she confirmed his original story about the blue coat, but not about his belief it was Tom he'd seen. Knowing Jake was out of the country, she wasn't concerned they would find out the rest. She watched them mutter and shake their heads at the lack of new evidence, and allowed a hint of a smile to cross her lips. Clearly dismissed by them, she would keep the additional information private. Nothing would stop her from finding the truth.

Chapter 12

After work, Aubrey stepped through her front door and heard the phone ringing. She picked up the receiver, and without preamble, her mother launched into her assault. "I understand you've accused Tom of killing your friend. What is wrong with you? Your brother is not capable of harming someone. He's very upset about you attacking him. You need to call and apologize to him right now."

The long cord on Aubrey's phone allowed her to wander around the living room, picking up old newspapers and empty glasses. She petted Kizzy as she half-heartedly listened to her mother's diatribe.

"Hello to you, too, Mom. Always happy to hear from you." She forced a chipper tone, while absently looking through her mail. *Hmmm, dog food coupons, I'll have to save those.*

"Don't you get smart with me, Aubrey. What do you have to say for yourself?"

"I'm sorry Tom is upset with me. You know what I do for a living. It's my job to ask questions, and he lied to me. I simply confronted him on his lies. And yes, it does implicate him. I'm trying to learn more and find out what really happened to Lori. I'm surprised he tattled on me to you."

Aubrey forced calmness in her voice belying her irritation. She settled herself on the couch and stretched out her legs.

"He did not *tattle* on you. He was hurt by what you said."

"I was hurt by his lies. Will you be sharing with him my disappointment about his dishonesty, and asking him to apologize to me?" She'd learned long ago not to argue or raise her voice. It got her nowhere, and only upset herself when she lost control.

"I'm sure he had a good reason to hold back with you. You're so abrasive and blunt, and you offend people with your lack of tactfulness. Calling someone and accusing them of *murder* is very unfair. Especially when it's your brother. Call him today and say you're sorry." Jayne hung up.

Aubrey looked at the silent phone. "Gosh, Mom, thanks for the moral support. Of course, I wouldn't expect anything less from you than criticism." She hung up the phone and seethed.

The phone rang again. Aubrey hesitated, thinking it might be her mother calling back. She sighed and grabbed the handset. "Hello?"

Nothing. Silence, followed by the sound of someone breathing.

"Who is this? Hello? Either speak, or I'll hang up." No response. She set the phone in its cradle, refusing to give any satisfaction to the caller by slamming it.

I wonder if that was my mystery man? Does he think it's intimidating to breathe into a phone? I should get a new number ... but he already knows where I live. She considered her options. *I need to let Sergeant Mills know ... or maybe the detectives instead. This could certainly be related to the recent murder.*

She picked up the phone and dialed the non-emergency line at the station. It rang several times before someone answered.

"Spencer Police, how can I direct your call?" a disembodied, but familiar, voice recited.

"Hi, Jack? This is Aubrey Stanton. Is Detective Brady or Weston available?"

"Hi, Aubrey. I think Brady's back there. I'll transfer you."

"Brady." A curt voice answered.

"Hi, Detective, this is Officer Stanton. I spoke with you yesterday about the Harris murder. I received a call a moment ago with someone breathing on the other end. I believe it's the same person who has called threatening me about the investigation. He could be the one that left the dead possum on my back door. I thought you should know, especially if ... "

"Yeah, I heard about that," he interrupted. "But I don't think it's related to the current case. I don't have time to deal with your *harasser*, Officer. I'm busy chasing leads on a *killer*. Talk to whoever's looking into the calls you've gotten." He hung up.

Well, that was rude. I wonder if he speaks to the public as harshly as he does to a fellow cop? What an asshole. She glanced around her living room. *I have to check the locks on my doors and windows. Then I need to go to Garrison Street and talk to the people near the park. So far, Tom's my only suspect.*

****

Aubrey walked the length of the block bordering the park. It would be getting dark in a couple hours, so she hurried between houses, trying to reach them all before calling it a day. Since Sergeant Mills had allowed her to only work the case when she was off-duty, she wore no uniform to identify herself. She was also officially no longer on the case, but no one would know that. If anyone asked, she'd show her identification. So far, no one had.

After speaking with over a dozen people and finding no new leads, she knocked on Richard Adams's door. Adams was a churlish sixty-three-year-old. His haircut and posture, despite his beer belly, vouched for a career in the Army or Marines. He stepped out of his house and stood ramrod straight on his perfect, orderly porch. Yellow and purple pansies peeked out of a window box on the railing as he listened to Aubrey explain who she was and why she was there. Adams asked to see her ID, and she held it up. *Whew, I almost didn't bring it ... almost didn't need it.*

"What makes ya think I saw anythin' I hadn't already told the police? That's what good citizens do, young lady," he replied in a prim, yet gravelly voice. His eyes scrutinized her face.

She bristled at the 'young lady' comment but chose to ignore it. "Mr. Adams, I understand you would have reported unusual activity, but I believe someone saw something and didn't realize what it was at the time. It may have looked like the girl was with someone she knew." Aubrey leveled her gaze at him.

"I'm not questioning your integrity, sir, I'm asking you to think back to any contact you may have witnessed between her and *anyone* else she may have been with."

"I did see a girl talkin' and laughin' with a boy in a blue coat, but the boy walked off, leavin' her alone. I told the police the same thing." His voice softened. "I went back to my roses. Ya can't be too careful with roses, ya know. They need constant attention if ya want to win the blue ribbon at the state fair."

Aubrey bit the inside of her cheek to stifle a laugh as he lowered his voice. Leaning toward her as if afraid the plants might hear him, Adams confided, "Bugs, like aphids or snails, can destroy 'em; diseases like black spot, powdery mildew, or the dreaded rose cankers, can ruin years of mulchin', feedin', and prunin.' I was dealin' with a mosaic virus on one of my prized plants, usually fatal, ya understand, but I had high hopes for it to survive, and, by golly, it did." He straightened his back and raised his chin, his face exuding pride over his accomplishment.

"It's wonderful you were able to save them. So ... how long were you out in your yard?"

"All afternoon. The only thing on the TV was 'bout Kennedy's upcoming campaign trip to Texas. Never liked the man, but it was a shame what happened to him."

"Yes, it was. Your yard is almost directly opposite of where the girl was found later. Are you sure you didn't see a car or truck stop and talk to her?"

"Hmm, now that ya mention it, there was a car, if ya can call it that." He lifted his hand and tapped his index finger against his lips as he concentrated. "A green Jeep Gladiator. Never seen one in person before, only in the ads in the paper ... brand new, too. That's why I noticed it. Ugly thing." He sneered. "Couldn't see the driver, I was on the wrong side. I say, if ya want to drive a military vehicle, join the service, like I did. OORAH!" When Aubrey startled, he explained, "That's the Marines yell. Twenty years in the Corps.

"Anyway, as I was sayin', the jeep pulled up alongside the girl, could hear they was talkin' but not what was said. I turned back to my blue-ribbon beauties, and when I looked up again, they was both gone. Ya figure, whoever was in that jeep, took her?"

"I don't know, sir, but I'll follow up on the information. It's something new to work with. Either I or someone else may be back to speak to you further about what you saw. Thank you for your service." Aubrey reached out to shake hands with him. "Your roses are beautiful. Good luck at the fair."

"Thank ya. I hope it helps." He shook her hand and retreated into the house.

This is a good lead. It gets Tom off the hook, as well. Time to go home and write it up. I wonder if I should let Tom know, or let him stew for a few days. Might bring him down a peg or two. Although Mom'll be full of 'I told you so.'

****

Wednesday morning, before going on patrol, Aubrey called her best friend, Donna. Michigan uses over a hundred branches of the Secretary of State's office, instead of a DMV, to handle vehicle registrations and driver's licenses. Donna worked for almost four years at the SOS, with access to all of the state vehicle records. Something Aubrey had discovered came in handy, now and again.

"Hey, Donna. How's it going?"

"Hey, Sweetie. I'm good. What do you need?"

"What makes you think I need anything?" she feigned surprise at her friend's forthrightness. Donna knew her better than anyone, including her family.

"C'mon, you only call when you do. It's fine, how can I help?"

"Sorry. We *should* get together soon. It's been a while, hasn't it? Anyway, you're right. I'm looking for records for a '63 green Jeep Gladiator. I need to know who owned it from this area, back in '63. Can you access those records?"

Donna ignored the question. "Pete and I are having a barbeque on Memorial Day. Why don't you come over? It would be nice to catch up." She paused, then continued, "Yes, I can access those records, but it'll take a few days. They're stored in boxes in the basement. Do you only want the name of the owner back in '63, or do you also want the person's current address?"

"If you could get me both, I would love you forever."

"You already love me, but you would *owe* me forever, girl. I don't relish going down into the basement and rifling through dusty, old boxes. Not to mention the spiders and other creepy-crawlies slinking about. Ugh."

"You're right, I *would* owe you. I appreciate your willingness to battle the bugs to help me find a murderer. I would also love to come to your barbeque … if I'm not working that day. How are Pete and the kids?"

"They're terrific, although I swear my mother's threat of 'Wait until you have kids' has definitely come back to haunt me with my Amy. At three years old, she's a regular terror."

"Kids grow up and get better," Aubrey sympathized. "Hang in there. If I'm able to come, can I bring a friend?"

"Of course, you can bring a friend. A special friend?" she asked.

"Not sure yet. Thanks for checking those records for me. Talk to you later."

Aubrey left the station and found her squad car covered in broken eggs.

"What the hell? What moron did this to my car?" She surveyed the lot, looking for any lurkers playing a practical joke on her. Seeing no one around, she gingerly opened the driver's door. She slid inside, hoping to avoid sticky, egg-guts dripping onto the car seat or her uniform. "I guess my first stop is the car wash. Not how I wanted to start my day," she grumbled.

The department had an account at Posh Wash. Grateful it looked like a slow day, she drove into the entrance. She stepped out of the car so the attendant could get in. *He may as well clean the inside while he's at it.*

"So, who'd you piss off?" he joked.

Aubrey recognized Roger, a high school acquaintance, and laughed. "No telling. Seems like I piss off plenty of people daily. I hope you can clean 'er up for me."

"No problem. I'll even make it smell nice."

He cleaned the inside while the automated machine scoured the outside. Aubrey wandered the displays in the waiting room, wondering if she should buy an air freshener for her Mustang. Before she decided, she saw Roger waving for her to come outside.

Retrieving the shiny, clean car, Aubrey tipped him and drove out. *Time to get to work, finally.* Her first call sent her to a domestic dispute in the older section of the city.

"All available units, domestic disturbance in progress at 486 High Street."

"Car forty-one responding," Aubrey replied. *I hate domestics. You never know what might happen.*

"Ten-four, car forty-one."

Dispatch relayed the escalating level of danger.

Aubrey raced across town, with lights blazing and siren blaring.

"Caller states boyfriend is threatening to kill her. States she is leaving the house. Receiving multiple calls from neighbors."

"Roger that. Car forty-one arriving on scene. Woman running out of a house toward the street."

"Ten-four. Back-up on the way."

Aubrey slammed on the brakes, threw the vehicle in park, flung open the door, and jumped out of her car.

A husky twenty-something man, approximately six feet tall, wearing beige cargo shorts, a dirty white tank top, and a red ball cap, burst out of the house. He aimed a twelve-gauge shotgun at the slim, petite woman who ran into the street, barefoot and screaming for help. Neighbors who'd been working or relaxing in their yards gathered to watch. One older man, who had been mowing his lawn, turned toward the noise and gawked at the sight.

Several people yelled at Aubrey, "Do something!"

Running toward the surreal scene, Aubrey drew her gun, and commanded, "Police, drop your weapon, drop it…"

Less than ten feet behind his fleeing girlfriend, the man fired into her retreating back. He dropped the shotgun and threw his hands in the air.

Back-up arrived with guns drawn. Aubrey rushed to check on the woman. The other officers yelled commands, ran to the man, knocked him to the ground, and handcuffed him. Aubrey yelled at another cop to radio for an ambulance. The woman's lungs had been struck by the buckshot, and bloody bubbles gurgled from her mouth. Aubrey held her, urging her to hold on.

The paramedics arrived too late to save her. The woman died … in the middle of the street … in a pool of blood.

One woman in the audience was screaming … and screaming … and screaming.

Someone shut her up!

Aubrey clenched her teeth and hands, struggling to maintain her composure in front of the crowd of onlookers. She had never experienced someone commit murder, right in front of her, while she watched in horror. Her fury at being too late and too slow overwhelmed her.

Spectators shrieked and cried. Some yelled, "Why didn't you shoot him?"

Why didn't I fire at him? Her eyes scanned the scene. *No, there were too many people around, I couldn't get a clear shot. What if I'd missed and hit a neighbor? No good choices or outcomes here.*

The newly-arrived paramedic checked the woman's pulse and covered her with a sheet. Aubrey strode back to her car and leaned against the hood, her left arm bracing her right elbow, trembling fingers spread across her mouth. Other officers surrounded the area with crime scene tape, and the lead detectives arrived. As the first officer on the scene, Aubrey stood up, strode over to them, and described what she had witnessed.

The street was chaos: neighbors wailing, shouting, shaking their fists. The woman's relatives descended with shocked expressions, moaned and keened, demanded answers. The news teams arrived within minutes. Reporters called out to her, shoving their microphones in her face. Aubrey ignored them and their insinuations. She returned to her patrol car, sat inside with the door ajar, and stared at nothing.

Lost in mentally reliving the incident, she didn't hear the other officers talking nearby, until one voice sliced through her sadness and outrage. Scott Fuller, loud and obnoxious, expressed his unsolicited opinions on the incident to a small group of cops huddled around him.

"She probably deserved it. Maybe she refused to give him a blow job, and he went off on her. What a stupid bitch."

He laughed, and his minions chuckled hesitantly, eyes jumping around the scene.

Aubrey leaped out of her car, strode over to Fuller, and with every ounce of her strength, punched him in the face. The officers standing near him attempted to grab her, but her intense and furious glare warned them off. She pointed her finger at Scott as he lay on the ground.

"No one deserves to be gunned down in the street." Fighting to control her volume, she continued, "But you need to check your mouth, asshole. There are neighbors here, family members, listening to your crap. Show some decency if you have any."

Her colleagues stepped back to give her space. As she turned and stormed away, she heard a few spectators cheering and clapping. One voice shouted, "You tell 'im, Officer."

Oh, great. I hate how he makes me lose control. I thought I had gotten so good at pretending he didn't get to me. Even if the audience appreciated it.

Back in her squad car, she drove off, heedless of the blood spatter on her sleeve. Working on autopilot, she wrote tickets for the next half hour, but was easily swayed into forgiveness by most of the minor traffic offenders.

Chapter 13

Sergeant Mills ordered Aubrey back to the station when he learned of the incident between her and Fuller. Walking toward Mills's office, she passed Scott, who had left it a moment before. He shot daggers at her, his hands clenched into fists. She couldn't miss the shiner she'd given him and pressed her lips together to avoid smirking.

"What the hell were you thinking, Stanton?" Mills bellowed at her, as she entered and closed the door.

"Did they tell you what he was doing? Demeaning the woman whose boyfriend shot her down in the street. And within earshot of her family and others there. I regret having lost my temper, but he needed to know his behavior and comments were offensive," Aubrey shouted back at him.

"*Your* behavior was offensive, also. You're lucky Fuller's not pressing charges against you for assault and battery. I can't have my officers fighting in the street. You're both suspended for a week." As she started to respond, he stopped her words with a scowl. "Be glad it's not a month."

His eyes softened, and he sighed. "As your sergeant, I have to reprimand you, but as a reasonable person, I commend you for stepping in, but you should have *told* him to stop, not *hit* him. Go get your hand checked out, it looks like you broke a knuckle, or two. Didn't anyone ever teach you how to punch? Keep your fingers tight, thumb tucked across them next time … and by next time, I don't mean a fellow officer." He jerked his head to indicate the door. "Get your uniform cleaned, it has blood on it. Now, get out of here. Do something useful with your time off."

Aubrey contained her smile until she was in the restroom, changing out of her uniform. The adrenaline coursing through her body had prevented her from realizing how much her swollen hand throbbed. She knew she shouldn't have hit Scott, but he deserved it. It felt good to have released all her anger and frustration. *Maybe I should go to the gym more often. Let off some steam.*

She gathered her uniform to take to the dry cleaners on her way home. *I wish Scott would act like a decent human being instead of a jerk. I wonder if he even knows how to be nice to anyone. Hmm, I wonder if he's nice to his mom.*

Leaving the station, she drove to an urgent care facility. They x-rayed, wrapped her hand to prevent movement, suggested ice, and gave her a prescription for pain. Her next stop was the pharmacy, where she picked up her medication, dropped off her uniform at the cleaners, and went home. She soon discovered the difficulty of doing anything with the fingers of her right hand immobilized.

I think I'll take one of those pain pills, put an ice pack on my hand, and take a nap. Haven't done that in a long time.

Within minutes, Aubrey fell asleep on the couch. Loud knocking on her front door woke her two hours later. She stumbled, half-asleep to look through the peephole. It was Brad.

Oh, no, I forgot about our date. She opened the door, motioning for him to enter.

"Hi, Brad." She gave him a brief hug. "I'm sorry. So much happened today, I forgot we had a date tonight. Come, sit down." She flopped onto the couch, yawning, as he sat on the edge of a chair opposite her.

"Are you okay?" His eyebrows furrowed as he observed Aubrey. "What happened to your hand?" He jumped up to look at it, but she waved him away.

"It's a long story, but basically, I punched someone, another cop. I broke two of my knuckles on his face and didn't even notice it."

His forehead creased, and he frowned. "Why?"

"He's been harassing me from day one in the academy, and today was the day he crossed a line. I couldn't let him get away with it." She scowled as she recalled Scott's words.

Brad's nostrils flared, and he gritted his teeth, eyes pierced through her. He growled, "What did he do, Aubrey? Did he ... assault you?"

Confusion danced across her face. Her forehead crinkled, and her lips pursed as she considered the question. "Huh? No ... no, he was acting like a jackass at a murder I responded to." She took a breath. "His name is Scott, and he showed up after a guy shot his girlfriend. I watched it happen. I was too slow to stop him. I can't get it out of my head. I'm still in shock ... and angry I couldn't prevent it."

She covered her face with her hands, hiding her unbidden tears. "And right now, I'm little fuzzy from the pain pills they gave me for my hand."

Brad sat next to her and shook his head. He hesitated and looked at Aubrey. "I'm lost here. You punched a guy in the face because he was acting like a jackass in public?" His voice echoed the skeptical look on his face.

"Yeah. He said the woman deserved to be shot because she probably refused to give her boyfriend a blow-job. He was laughing about it, and there were neighbors and her relatives standing within hearing distance. After I hit him, the crowd cheered." She groaned and winced in pain.

"I still don't understand why you felt you had to hit him instead of telling him to be quiet. Is that how you usually react to things you don't agree with? With violence? Did they fire you?"

She closed her eyes for a moment, resigned to try again. "I'm not explaining this right, and you don't know this guy. It was an accumulation of two years' worth of his ass-ness ... is that a word? I'm sorry, but I don't feel very well. Can we do a raincheck?"

"Of course, we can. Why don't you lie down, and I'll let myself out." His words curt. "I'll call you tomorrow."

"Thanks, and no, they didn't fire me, a one-week suspension."

Aubrey looked at him with a cheesy grin. "The good news is that I'll be available all day for a while if you'd like to hang out." She laid down, curling up with a blanket.

He half-smiled and gave her a peck on the cheek. "Get some rest." He walked out the door, locking it as he went.

****

Aubrey woke up the next morning, stiff and sore from sleeping all night on the couch. She stretched and flexed before her toast and juice breakfast. She showered as best she could with her dominant hand impaired. Dressed in jeans and a polo, Aubrey looked around and realized she'd planned nothing for the day.

"What should we do, Kizzy?" The little dog sat, cocked her head, tongue lolling, eyes alert. "It's too hard to clean or do laundry with this hand. I'm fresh out of leads on Lori's killer until I get the information from Donna on the Jeep owner. Maybe I should try to make it up to Brad for last night and invite him to lunch."

Kizzy yipped her agreement and did a little doggy boogie.

She dialed his number and waited.

"Hello?" a woman's sultry voice answered.

"I'm sorry. I must have the wrong number. I was calling for Brad."

The voice shifted from sultry to perky. "Oh, sure, Brad's here."

What is going on? Who is she?

"Hello?"

Not sure how to continue, or whether to ask who answered his phone, she chose a standard greeting. "Um, hi, Brad, this is Aubrey. How are you?"

"Hi, Bree. I'm good. How are you feeling? Did you get some sleep?"

His voice was cheerful, not furtive or annoyed, so she asked, "Yes, I did, thanks. Who was that who answered the phone? I thought you lived alone."

He chuckled. "I do live alone. That was my big sister."

Aubrey heard the woman in the background yell, "Not BIG ... older, wiser sister, you idiot." Brad laughed and shouted back, "Yes, much older, possibly wiser." To Aubrey, he said, "Sorry, that's Aster, short for Astragal. She's my twin, born four minutes before me."

"That's an unusual name."

"Our dad's a carpenter and named us for building materials; me, Brad as in a brad nail, and her, Astragal for a type of molding strip. Family joke, I guess."

"That's kinda funny, actually. You never mentioned a sister, much less a twin. I don't remember her from school."

"No, she didn't go to Spencer. She's a world-class equestrian and went to a riding academy in Virginia instead of regular high school. She got all the athletic prowess, I got the brains."

Again, in the background, Aubrey heard Aster shout, "Yeah, right."

"Ignore her," he said and raised his volume, "she's leaving now. What's going on?"

"Sorry, I didn't know you had company. I was going to invite you to lunch to make up for last night."

"That sounds great, and as I was saying, she's leaving. She stopped by to borrow my truck. She's hauling grain and hay to her horse out in Troy. Aster likes him to have a special kind, and the place where she boards him won't supply it. Once a month, she stocks up, so he gets what she wants."

"Okay, would you like to meet me at Kelly's, or I can pick you up if she has your truck?"

"I can meet you. Kelly's is good, and remember, I have a car, too. She'll have the truck for a couple of days before bothering to return it to me. What time?"

"Say, one o'clock?"

"Cool, see you there."

****

Brad and Aubrey pulled into the restaurant's lot at the same time, parked, and met at the door. Kelly's was an Irish pub that had morphed from an old convenience store of the same name. The owners tore down the original building to appease the upscale residents of a high-end housing development nearby. The fixtures and seating were relatively new and sleek, but the food was old-fashioned grub: sandwiches, cottage pie, corned beef and cabbage, hamburgers, and the like, a combination of Irish and American fare and drinks. The clientele: a mixture of horse people, farmers, and country club nouveau riche. The original store's hitching post still stood outside, and occasionally, so did a horse.

They hugged and went inside, took a table in the corner, and picked up the menus.

"That must be fun, having a twin," Aubrey said, as they waited for their server.

"Sometimes, but she never lets me forget she was born first." He grimaced.

Aubrey smiled at the new version of baby brother Brad. "Sometimes being the youngest has its advantages, and sometimes, not. I got a call from my mother chastising me for hurting my brother's feelings. No concern for how he hurt mine first." She shook her head.

"Funny how mothers protect their sons, and fathers, their daughters." He paused a beat, realized his misstep. "Oh, man, I always put my foot in my mouth when I'm around you. Sorry, I didn't mean to bring up your dad."

"It's okay. My dad was not the protective type, and we weren't close. I kind of miss him. But it's weird." She shrugged her shoulders. "Here comes our server, do you know what you want?"

The server took their orders, a club sandwich for Brad and a chef's salad with fries for Aubrey, and brought their drinks. The conversation shifted back to Brad's sister.

"So, your sister, Aster, how did she become this excellent equestrian?"

"She was always a horse nut. When we were little, she had toy horses, instead of dolls, and spent her time creating elaborate jumping courses for them. Her horse naturally won." He snorted. "She was the only competitor, though, so it was a given. She's been obsessed forever, and my parents took her for riding lessons when she was five. She's a gifted horsewoman and has won international hunt and hack events, even a steeplechase or two."

"Not sure what all that is, but it sounds amazing."

Brad laughed. "Hack and hunt are dressage, kind of like horse obedience, and jumping. Steeplechases are cross-country races."

"That sounds exciting. And you, Brad? What are you accomplished at? I'm guessing your parents didn't leave you on the sidelines, did they?"

Aubrey was happy he had more involved parents than she did, but also a bit envious about all she'd missed. She couldn't change the way things were, but she could choose to be a better mother someday than her own.

"I *am* athletic, truth be told, but I'm not a jock. I prefer to use my head for thinking instead of a target to be bashed in. I played hockey, but after I lost my first tooth to a puck, I quit. And you?"

"Well, I'm pretty good at lots of things, but not excellent at much. As a kid, I bowled, ice- skated, rode horses, roller- skated, played tackle football, and pitched for the neighborhood baseball team. I took a little karate and judo after high school and loved the karate part, even if I never got past a yellow belt. The training came in handy at the academy."

"That's impressive. I better watch my step, right?" Brad teased. "It's good to have lots of different skills, I think. Better than excelling in one to the detriment of everything else."

His face turned serious. "Aubrey, I do have some questions about what happened yesterday. I'm concerned about your reaction to that guy's rudeness. I know you said it was a culmination of events and harassment, but don't you think you took it too far, by punching him?"

Aubrey took a deep breath, settling her annoyance. *It's really none of his business, but I like Brad, and I want to be open and honest with him.*

"Yes, I did. There was no excuse for hitting Scott, even if he was being an insensitive jerk. My sergeant told me I crossed a line, which is why I was suspended. Fuller was, too. It won't happen again. I was overwhelmed by watching that poor woman get shot in the back by someone she'd trusted. Coming on the heels of my father's fatal car accident, and the murder case I've re-opened, his comments infuriated me. I overreacted."

"Okay, I think I understand. I'm glad you realize you were wrong." His words sounded smug to Aubrey. "I've never dated a cop before. I knew violence was part of the job ... but maybe it carries over into your personal life. I've never hit a person, so it was a shock to hear you had."

"Police work can be violent, frequently is, in fact, but that doesn't mean *I'm* a violent person. I don't need you to judge me, Brad. You don't know me that well." Her eyes bore into his, and she gritted her teeth. Her pulse raced. She could handle confrontation on the job, but between friends, it unnerved her.

He watched her jaw tighten and eyes narrow. "Jeez, Aubrey, you're giving me a 'cop look.' Are you angry? I would hope you could understand my apprehension, not turn on me."

To control the shaking of her hands, Aubrey studied her wilting salad and chilly fries on her plate. She looked up, unclenched her teeth, and raised her eyebrows in a conciliatory expression. "My work has been a sore point with nearly every boy, or man, I've dated. I'm getting used to it. If you aren't comfortable with what I do for a living, say so, but don't second-guess my actions.

"You weren't there, and you haven't been through what I have. I don't expect you to completely understand, but I hoped you were capable of listening and discussing events and ideas, without the self-righteousness." She waggled her eyebrows, and one side of her mouth crooked up into a wry grin. "After all, I thought you were going to be a lawyer, not a judge."

He laughed. "I call a truce. I care about you, Bree, and don't want to fight. I'm sure this was a one-time thing, and I'd like to move past it if you can."

Her stomach relaxed. "Any time you have concerns again, please tell me. I'm only asking that we talk about it, not jump to conclusions. Deal?"

"Deal."

Chapter 14

Aubrey took advantage of the time off work while she waited to hear from her friend, Donna, about the Jeep Gladiator's owner information. She and Brad walked their dogs in the park, went to the movies, and enjoyed each other's company. Each learned more about the other person's likes and dislikes. To Aubrey's delight, they had quiet, intimate time, as well. No sex yet, but she believed it was on the horizon.

Donna called early Monday morning. "Aubrey, I have the owner's name for that jeep you were interested in. There was only one sold in this area. The rest were either way up north, like in Cadillac, in the Upper Penninsula, or out of state, at least at the time Lori was killed. Besides, most weren't green, so that narrowed it down, too. It was registered to an Oliver Larson, right here in Spencer. I found out the jeep was sold almost ten years ago. Larson is dead, so I wasn't able to get a current address, of course. Unless you want his cemetery plot number." She laughed, then apologized. "I'm sorry, I know this is important to you, but if this was your guy, it isn't the same one who killed Erin Grant."

Aubrey gasped. "Erin Grant? She's the one they found dead a week ago? I've been off work and haven't been watching the news. I hadn't heard they'd identified her. Are you sure?"

"Yeah, I'm sure. She was nineteen and lived in town. Did you know her?"

"No, but her name is familiar. Thanks for the information on the jeep. You're the best. I appreciate it. I'll get back to you about the barbeque. I gotta go. Bye."

Aubrey took several deep breaths, as her thoughts swirled and her stomach heaved. She ran to the bathroom and lost her breakfast.

Erin? Tom was flirting with her at Dad's funeral. He went out that night. I have no idea where, and two days later, she's discovered dead in the park. I thought I'd cleared Tom with Adams's statement.

She rinsed out her mouth and sat on the toilet lid, considering what she had heard and how it fit together. *Tom couldn't have done it, he was gone before Erin was found. Unless he can transport a body through telekinesis from California, it can't be him ... unless he has a partner here.*

Aubrey took a shower, dressed, grabbed a breakfast bar, and slipped into her car. She drove to the high school, checked in at the office, and walked to the library. At the front desk, she asked the librarian, Mrs. Hughes, to see the school yearbooks from 1961 through 1965.

Starting in 1961, she flipped to the index in the back, looking for Oliver Larson. She found him on the senior class list. *He would have been twenty years old in 1963. Old enough to be driving his own car. But would he have known Tom? Tom was only twelve.*

She absently glanced around the room. *I can't see a twenty-year-old hanging out with a twelve-year-old. Hmmm, Jake was six years older than Lori, so he would have been fourteen at the time. Again, too young to be spending time with a guy six years older. Another dead end.*

Aubrey returned the books to Mrs. Hughes and left, disappointed. Deep in thought, she almost ran into Miss Olsen, the Spanish teacher, coming around the corner.

"Oh, Miss Olsen, I'm so sorry. I wasn't watching where I was going."

The teacher laughed. "We seem to do that a lot, don't we? Running into each other. What brings you to the school today, Aubrey?"

"I'm still working on Lori Harris's case. Trying to track down a guy who drove a green jeep back in 1963. I mean, I found him, but I actually was trying to find a connection to someone else through him."

"Hmm, a green jeep?" She tapped her lips with her index finger. "I recall one of my former students driving one, maybe a year or two after graduation. It was pretty distinctive, and hideous, if I do say so myself." She tsked and shook her head. "One of the reasons I noticed it."

She furrowed her brow, concentrating, and looked at Aubrey. "Oliver Larson, that's who it was. I saw him frequently when he dropped someone off in the mornings. Maybe he had a younger brother? Or maybe a slightly younger friend? I didn't recognize the young man. Sorry. But I know you'll get to the bottom of this."

"I appreciate your faith in me, but I keep running into roadblocks."

"Keep working at it. It'll come. It's important to ask the right questions." Miss Olsen patted Aubrey's arm and walked off.

Aubrey hurried back to the library. *Thank you, Miss Olsen. Let's see who his friends and possibly relatives were.*

"Hi. I need those yearbooks again. Sorry to be a bother." She smiled at Mrs. Hughes.

"Of course. It's no bother at all. I hadn't had a chance to put them back, anyway. Here you go."

Aubrey took the books and sat at a table away from the few students studying in the room. She flipped open the 1961 yearbook and looked at the index. There were no other Larsons listed. *So, no younger brothers. Maybe a friend?* She looked for Oliver again and found his list of activities: football, baseball, basketball, ski club ... *A real jock, wasn't he?*... National Honor Society, Science Club. *Ah, ha! Let's start with the Science Club.*

She turned to a listing of the club members, running her finger down the names. She found Oliver Larson with no problem but couldn't determine who his friends were. She glanced at the photos of some of the kids in groups doing experiments or showing off their projects.

One face caught her eye. It looked familiar. There were four boys in the picture, the caption identified them. A good-looking, blond-haired boy was Larson, next was Dan Hunter, with a goofy smile on his face, Greg Wyatt, and Jaime Harris, whose face was familiar because he looked like a lesser version of his brother, Jake.

Oh, my God, they were all friends, or at least knew each other. Who was he picking up and dropping off, though? Jaime was a freshman in '61. She checked the index for Greg Wyatt. *He was a sophomore. So, in 1963, Greg wouldn't need a ride ... he was due to graduate, but Jaime might not have been driving yet. He wouldn't kill his own sister, though, or condone anyone else doing it. At least I can't imagine that. And who is the goofy-looking kid, Dan Hunter?*

The index didn't link Hunter, a freshman, to any of the others except in that one picture. *I can't rule him out, regardless.*

After returning the books to the librarian, Aubrey drove home. She walked in and opened the hall closet, where she stashed her phone book. Opening the book to W, Aubrey scanned down to Wyatt. There were seven listed, none of them Greg or G. Starting with Brian Wyatt's number, she dialed and waited.

"Hello?"

"Hi, my name is Aubrey Stanton, and I'm looking for an old classmate of mine, Greg Wyatt? Is he a relation of yours, by any chance?" she asked.

"Sorry, no. There aren't any Gregs in the family, and besides, we're new to the city."

"Okay, thanks, sorry to bother you." She hung up. Dialed the next one, and the next five. Same story, same basic answer, no one by that name. She struck paydirt on the last one.

"Hello?'

Aubrey went through her spiel for the seventh time. Her upbeat tone starting to fade.

"Yes, he is," a friendly, female voice replied. "Why are you looking for him?"

She repeated her false story, "We're planning a class reunion and trying to track down as many people as we can. Do you have his phone number or address so I can let him know?"

"Well, I guess there's no harm in sharing that. My son, Greg, lives in California now, though, so he probably won't be able to come here for it. When is it? I could pass the information along."

Aubrey avoided agreeing to have her tell Greg about the pretend reunion. "Really? California? My older brother lives there. Where does Greg live?"

"Um, in Minnie ... no, that's not right ... Minerva. That's it. My memory is awful these days, old age, you know. Don't ever get old, honey. It's not a lot of fun," the woman grumbled, then laughed. "It's better than the alternative, though. My husband, Greg's father, passed away two years ago, and that's the last time I saw Greg. He doesn't come home as often as I'd like these days." Her voice quavered. "I guess he's too busy working in the mines there. Says he's going to be a millionaire when he strikes gold. I don't have a lot of faith in that happening."

"I understand. I don't see my brother as often as I'd like either. I'm sorry to hear about your husband. Would you happen to know if Greg was friends with Dan Hunter?" Aubrey held her breath.

"Hmmm, Dan Hunter ... oh, yes, one of the Hunters who lives on Cleveland Street. His father is a lawyer. Dan and Greg weren't really friends, but they knew each other."

"Do you know if he's still around?"

"I think he's working for his dad at the firm in town. Hunter, Chase and Hook. Cute, huh?"

Aubrey laughed. "I've heard of them but never had a reason to visit the office. Is Dan a lawyer? He seems too young."

"Yes, he is young. He's still in school, works as a clerk for his dad, getting some experience, I think is all. Let me get you Greg's information, but I'm pretty sure he won't come to the reunion. I wish he would. Maybe I'd get a chance to see him, too." She sounded wistful.

Aubrey jotted down the information, and asked, "Before you go, would you know if Greg was friends with Oliver Larson?"

"Absolutely, they were best friends. Ollie even sold him his jeep. Greg said it was a steal. Almost brand new, but butt-ugly. I never understood why he wanted that thing. It was a shame when Ollie died. So sad. The cancer got him ... he was so young. Greg was devastated. I think that's why he moved away." Her voice choked. "Anyway, thanks for calling. I'll tell Greg you're looking for him."

Aubrey thanked Mrs. Wyatt and hung up. In a murmur, she reviewed what she'd discovered. "So, Tom and Greg live and work in Minerva in the mining business. Dan works in his father's law office, and Oliver is dead but was best friends with Greg. That's who he was picking up, I'll bet. Greg must not have been driving or didn't own a car until Larson sold him the jeep. Now, how does Jaime Harris, living in Oregon, fit into this picture?"

Chapter 15

With only one day left of her suspension for hitting Scott Fuller, Aubrey called Mrs. Harris as early as she felt was acceptable.

"Mrs. Harris, this is Aubrey. How are you today?" She used a soft opening before revealing the real questions she had for Lori's mother.

"I'm fine, dear. Have you learned anything new about Lori?"

Well, so much for starting the conversation off slowly.

"I'm following up on some leads, and I'm hoping you can help with a little background. I'm looking into the relationships between some boys I've come across during my research. I know Jaime graduated in 1965, and perhaps he was too young to know them, but I thought I'd ask. I found a picture of him with three other boys from the Science Club: Oliver Larson, Greg Wyatt, and Dan Hunter. Do any of these names ring a bell for you, as Jaime's friends, perhaps?"

"Do you think one of these boys could have killed Lori?" Her horrified reply came through loud and clear over the phone line.

Aubrey promptly reassured her, "No, ma'am. I don't have any reason to believe so. I'm simply following up on some new information and timelines."

She heard the woman take a deep breath and exhale. "Well, okay. Greg Wyatt sounds familiar, but I don't think I ever met him, so he couldn't have been one of my son's close friends. I've never heard of Oliver Larson." She paused. "Now, I know Dan Hunter's name, but perhaps that's because of his father's law firm in town. Would you like me to call Jaime and ask?"

"I appreciate the offer, but if it's okay with you, I'd like to call him myself. As I said, I need to clear up some timelines."

"Of course. I'm sure Jaime'd be happy to help. Here's his phone number." She recited the number to Aubrey. "He doesn't always answer his phone. He lives in a commune out in Oregon, and I think they work a lot, growing their own food and such. So many young people are doing that these days. Don't want to be part of our society. I don't understand it, but if he's happy.... If you leave him a message, he'll call you back. Was there anything else?"

"Not at this time. Thanks so much, Mrs. Harris. Every tiny detail helps."

"Call any time, Aubrey. Have a good day."

Aubrey looked at the clock. *Ten o'clock, too early to call Oregon, it would be ... seven? I'll wait until noon when it'll be nine out there. Hopefully, he'll answer his phone. I doubt the department would give me plane fare to go interview him.* She snorted at the ludicrous idea. *I can't call Greg, either, since it's the same time in California.*

She doodled some stick people on the edge of her notepad, labeling and drawing connecting lines. *I'd like to talk to Dan Hunter, but I don't want to waltz into an attorney's office to ask questions that might implicate him in a crime.* She rubbed her thumb against her bottom lip. *Maybe I'll drive over there at quitting time and try to catch him outside, suggest getting a drink. This detective work is harder than I thought. Inexperience and lack of training, I guess.* She shrugged. *That's okay, I'll figure it out, one step at a time.*

With the better part of the day ahead of her, Aubrey returned to the urgent care clinic to have her hand checked.

"The X-ray looks good, Aubrey. Your knuckles are healing well, but you still have to be careful for the next two weeks. I suggest you have physical therapy to improve your grip strength, finger strength, and range of motion. Wait another week, and you can call a therapist, or we can set it up for you. Be gentle with it in the meantime." The doctor palpated for soreness and sent her on her way.

Injuries were not new to her, having broken other bones playing various sports, but this was her gun hand. She returned home and put ice on her knuckles, worried they might swell without the wrapping. Aubrey settled in to plan her questions for Dan Hunter. It was eleven-thirty. She had time to work on them before calling Greg. Recalling Miss Olsen's advice, asking the right questions was her top priority. She debated how to begin her line of questioning and pulled out a fresh sheet of paper.

Start with basic questions, like, did you know Oliver and Greg? Jaime? How well? Did you have any concerns about any of them? "No, that's crap. I need to get him relaxed and bring their names up more indirectly."

Aubrey tapped her pencil tip against the paper, creating a dotted maze. *Maybe I can use the phony reunion story to fish for info, invite him for a drink. What if Dan won't go have a drink with me, then what? Start yelling my questions at him as he drives off?* She laughed at how ridiculous it sounded. *I guess I'll have to play it by ear... again.*

At noon, she dialed Greg's phone number, listened to it ring at the other end.

"Hello?"

"Hi, this is Aubrey Stanton from Spencer. Is this Greg Wyatt?"

"Yeah, are you Tom's sister?"

I should have expected that, but didn't. It's a small town there.

"Um, yes, it is. Do you have a minute to talk, Greg?"

"A minute. I'm in the middle of something here. What do you need?"

He's kind of abrupt, isn't he? She furrowed her brow and chose a more professional manner.

"Tom may have mentioned I'm a police officer, and I'm investigating Lori Harris's murder. I have some questions for you. Trying to tie up loose ends. I spoke with your mother, and she said you were best friends with Oliver Larson. Is that correct?"

"Yeah, what of it?" Aubrey heard the change in tone. His response sounded more hostile than she anticipated.

"I understand he used to pick you up and drop you off at school, even after he'd graduated." *A little white lie, since I didn't actually know that.*

"He did. We were best friends. I didn't own a car until he sold me his jeep."

"A witness said he saw Oliver's jeep near the park the day Lori Harris was reported missing, and someone was talking with her out the driver's window. Were you with him?"

His tone turned brusque. "No. I don't know what you're talking about."

"It was after school. Lori was walking alone through the park and stopped on Garrison Street to speak with someone in a green Jeep Gladiator. Are you sure he didn't mention it to you?"

"No, he never said anything. Besides, she was little, why would either of us bother with a kid?"

Good point. Most teenage boys wouldn't unless they were teasing her. I certainly received my fair share of that behavior.

"That's what I'm trying to find out." *I'll try giving him an out here.* "Why would Oliver be talking to her ... unless, were you and Oliver friends with Jaime, Lori's brother? Maybe he was offering her a ride home, along with Jaime? Could he have picked him up as well as you, Greg?"

"I already told you, I wasn't with him. I have no idea if Jaime was or not. I gotta go." He disconnected the call.

He didn't say Oliver wasn't friends with Jaime. Something's fishy here. Tom must have warned him I might call, but why? Sounds like they're closing ranks. I need to call Jaime and hope they haven't already contacted him. She banged her fist in frustration on the table. "What did I expect? That they would roll over on each other? My inexperience showing its ugly claws again."

She called the number Mrs. Harris had given her, but it rang and rang. No answering machine, so she couldn't leave a message. *I'll try calling again later.* She gritted her teeth and held back her anger. She looked down at Kizzy's doggie grin and couldn't help smiling, relieving some pent up irritation.

She patted her little friend's head and spoke aloud. "Maybe I'm not very good at this. I probably should have waited until I had more time on the job before pursuing something seasoned detectives couldn't figure out." Exasperated, she sat and tapped her fingers on the table. "I can't give up now. Lori deserves better than my self-pity."

Her stomach growled. Aubrey patted it and made a bologna and cheese sandwich, found a bag of potato chips and took a cola from the fridge, then sat at the table to eat. Her mind raced with the details she'd discovered, but she managed to wait until she completed her lunch before launching her review of the facts she'd learned.

Aubrey grabbed a legal pad to make a list of the connections between people. Her stick people doodles from earlier gave her a start.

1. Oliver and Greg were best friends.
2. Two years after graduation, Oliver drops off/picks up Greg from school.
3. Oliver, Greg, Jaime, and Dan all knew each other through the Science Club.

4. Oliver's jeep spotted at last known location of Lori in the park on Monday.

5. Greg claims he wasn't in the jeep when it was seen with Lori.

6. Greg doesn't deny Jaime being friends with him and Oliver.

7. Greg works with and knows Tom, lives in the same small town.

8. Oliver sold jeep to Greg, then died.

9. Tom in town the night Erin goes missing, but gone before she's found dead two days later.

By the time Aubrey had listed and re-listed her salient connections, crossed out, and added various details, it was four-thirty. Time to catch Dan coming out of work. She changed into a sexier blouse to grab his attention. *Maybe this isn't very professional, but I need him to talk to me.* She jumped into her car. Aubrey figured she may have to wait until five, but didn't really know what time he left work. When she arrived, the parking lot was empty. She parked her car and walked to the door. A sign indicated the office closed at four-thirty.

Goddamnit! What a dummy I am. I should have called and at least found out what the office hours were. Waste of time. Now I have to try again tomorrow, right after my shift. Or... I could try calling him at home, ask if he'd meet me. But, under what pretense? If he's involved at all, he won't, and I'll have tipped him off. If he's not involved, he won't have anything to say, so more wasted time. I need to talk to Steve.

Aubrey stopped at a Jack-in-the-Box, ordered three tacos and a Coke from the drive-thru, headed home, and changed clothes. She hadn't realized how hungry she was until she sat at her kitchen table to eat. After cleaning up the empty wrappings, she called her friend, former police detective, Steve Rollins.

"Hey, Steve, it's Aubrey. How are you?"

"I'm good, thanks. What's up?"

"I've found some things out about the day Lori went missing. I was wondering if I could stop by. Maybe you'd see something I don't, or send me in the right direction." *I'll need to share what I suspect about Tom if I want his help. This could get sticky.* She grimaced at the thought of betraying her brother.

"Sure. I'm finishing dinner. Give me a half-hour?"

"Of course. How about I come by at six-thirty?"

"That'll work. See you."

****

Aubrey arrived at Steve's house, grabbed her legal pad off the passenger seat, and walked to his front door. He greeted her warmly and suggested, "Why don't we sit at the kitchen table where we'll have room to spread out your notes?"

"Good idea. How have you been?"

"Same old, same old. Not much to do when you're retired, if you don't play golf, that is." He chuckled. "Want something to drink?"

"No, thanks. I'm good." She sat in one of the French provincial wooden chairs and put her notepad on the table. "I think I'm onto something here, but I'm stuck. I'm hoping you can help unstick me, if you know what I mean? I can't talk to anyone at the station, and I'm asking you not to speak to anyone about what I show you unless we both agree it's the right course. Okay?"

"Of course. I'm delighted you're making headway on this. I thought at first I might be angry with myself for not finding whatever you have but decided time and fresh eyes can reveal new clues. Let's catch this bastard." Steve's predatory smile and narrowed eyes showed Aubrey how intense this former detective had been. It was a side of him she'd never seen before but was glad to have him in her corner.

Aubrey laid out her notes and graphs, summarized the conversations she'd had, and ended with her inability to figure out a way to approach Dan without alerting him to the connections she'd made.

"Wow, you've done some great work here. Finding Adams was a huge lead. I'm impressed with what you've done so far, Aubrey." She beamed at the high praise from her idol. "I agree, it's tough to know how far to go with someone who might be a witness or even a co-conspirator. The new death certainly muddies the water, too." He stood and pulled a beer out of the refrigerator. "Want one? Or something else?"

"If you have a cola, I'll take one. Thanks."

Steve sat back down and handed her the drink. "So why do you think Dan Hunter might be involved? Because he was in the Science Club with the other guys? Are you sure there's a bigger connection?"

Aubrey took a deep breath before admitting, "No, I'm not sure, but I think I need to eliminate him as a suspect. I think he might shed light on the relationship between the others as well. Do you think it's a waste of time with him?"

He sighed. "Police work is a lot of guessing and being wrong and wasting time, unfortunately. It's not like on TV, where they solve mysteries in an hour and in a linear fashion." Picking up one of her notes, he continued, "The fact that these young men are interconnected by several strands is not a coincidence. Knowing this Oliver owned the jeep Adams saw with Lori the day she disappeared, is a significant find. I would accept that he took her, but who was with him and who else knows what happened are the questions now. He's dead, so if the others all claim ignorance, it's a dead end. The problem is, is the recent murder of this new girl in a similar style. Is this a copycat, or one of Oliver's buddies who was involved the first time?"

"If we think Greg was involved the first time, how could he have been involved this time? He's in California. I hate to admit this, but my brother, Tom, was flirting with Erin Grant at my father's funeral. He and I got into an argument that evening about his leading her on. Then he went out that evening and came back after midnight." She winced. "If Tom is the doer this time, how did she end up in the park two days after he'd left? Even Jaime is in Oregon. The only one left in this group, who is still living here, is Dan."

"I hate to say it, but your brother was seen with Erin, the victim, the same day she went missing. You just admitted he went out alone that night and didn't come home until after midnight. Maybe he met up with Dan, and they killed her. He might have left Dan to handle the disposal after he'd left, thinking that would provide an alibi for him."

He furrowed his brow and pressed his lips together while he appeared to gather his thoughts. "I would treat Dan as a suspect and ask him where he was that night. Don't mention Tom's name to him. Find out where he lives and approach him at home, your ID in hand when you knock on the door. It will let him know it's an official visit. Be a cop, not a friend."

"That's great advice. I'm concerned that he will simply say he's not talking without an attorney if I come on too strong."

Steve appeared to consider her concerns. "Okay, take a recorder with you and let him know you have to use it to document everything. Tell him you're tying up loose ends on the investigation. Make sure he thinks he's in the clear but don't mention Erin, only Lori. Convince Hunter it's about the cold case, not the current one, and you're looking into the possibility of Oliver's complicity in Lori's murder. Say you only want to close the case for her parents and came across his name in connection to Oliver. You're dotting your I's and crossing your T's."

He downed the last of his beer and set the bottle on the counter before continuing.

"In other words, put him at ease. Watch his body language. When you ask him a question, look for fidgeting, eye-blinking, clenched jaw, as 'tells' that he's nervous. Don't provoke him, or you may inadvertently show your hand. People are sometimes so anxious to get things off their chests, they'll say all kinds of things you don't expect, *if* they see you as non-threatening. Sometimes the best bait is the one the fish doesn't see."

Chapter 16

After the meeting with Steve, Aubrey returned home to make a plan. She saw she'd missed a call and pressed the playback button.

"Hey, Aubrey, it's Jake. I wanted to tell you I remembered something else. Call me when you get a chance. I'm in a tiny town called Ouirgane, at the only hotel. Reception is sketchy, but it's the Hotel Soleil Imlil. The number is ..."

She grabbed a piece of paper and replayed the message to get the phone and room numbers correct. Realizing she had no idea what the time difference was, she called the telephone operator.

"There's a five hour time difference between Detroit, Michigan, and Morocco, Africa."

Aubrey smiled as she hung up the phone. Her heart raced in anticipation of a new lead. *I wouldn't mind chatting with Jake again, and, with any luck, he'll have additional information I can use. I'll have to call him in the morning, too late now.*

Her phone rang.

"This is Aubrey." She hoped it was Jake calling back, but it was his brother instead.

"Hi, this is Jaime ... Harris. My mom said you ... uh ... wanted to ... uh ... talk to me?"

Aubrey was surprised but happy he called since she'd not been able to leave a message for him before. He sounded stoned. She had enough experience with stoners to recognize their slow and halting cadence. She wasn't sure she could use whatever he told her but decided to go ahead.

"Hi, Jaime. Thanks for calling. Yes, I do have some questions for you about the day your sister disappeared. Do you have time now?" She consciously slowed her speech to mimic his.

"Yeah, I ... gueeessss."

"Great. I'm not sure what your mother told you, but I'm following up on some information I received recently and am hoping you can help. I have a witness who claims he saw Lori talking with a person in a green Jeep Gladiator the afternoon she went missing. Do you know who might have owned that car?"

"Suuurrrre, there was only one around. It was ... Ollie Larson's jeep."

"Were you friends with Ollie?"

"Kinda." He paused for several beats. "We hung out ... sometimes ... but weren't close friends. I guess he died ... a looong time ago."

"Weren't you still living here when that happened?"

"Yeeeaaah."

"You didn't go to the funeral?" It wasn't relevant, but her confusion caused her to blurt out the question.

"Nah." She heard him inhale and hold his breath, exhale, then continue. "Like I said, man, we weren't, like, friends."

"Okay. Do you recall a Greg Wyatt or Dan Hunter?"

"Greg was my best friend." He paused again, coughed. "I knew Dan ... but didn't hang out with him."

Aubrey rubbed her forehead. *Greg was supposed to be best friends with Oliver. I wonder if Jaime really remembers things clearly.* "Did Ollie ever pick you up after school?"

"Once in a while. Why?"

"Do you remember if you were with him the day Lori disappeared?"

"No."

Hmmm, he sounds more curt and lucid than a moment ago.

"No, you don't remember, or no, you weren't with him?" Aubrey asked.

"No, I wasn't with him."

"Do you recall if Greg or Dan were with him that day? Maybe, you saw them in the jeep after school?"

"No."

"Okay. Thanks for your time. Is there a better phone number if I need to speak to you again? The one your mother gave me didn't have an answering machine hooked up."

"No. Sorry, man. I gotta go." He hung up.

Well, that was strange. Jaime sounded like he was completely out of it until the end. I wonder if he smoked weed back in school and truly can't remember, or if he's protecting himself or someone else. Maybe Jake can help tomorrow.

****

Aubrey's alarm woke her at five the next morning, and she immediately called Jake's number.

"Hotel Soleil Imlil. How can I help you?" a woman's smooth, lilting French accent answered.

"Hello. May I have Room 9, please?"

"One moment."

"It's a wonderful morning in Africa. This is Jake."

"Hey, Jake. This is Aubrey. You sound quite cheerful this morning." She smiled, imagining him in his room. *He has the most beautiful smile ... and other things.*

"Oh, hi. Glad you called. I am cheerful. I have an assignment in the bush later, photographing hyenas. I also have some possible information for you, but I'm not happy about *it*."

"That sounds intriguing. What's up?"

"After our last conversation, I started thinking back to the day Lori disappeared. At the time, it didn't register for me how strangely Jaime acted that night. He was agitated and refused to eat dinner. I recall my mother wondering out loud what was going on with him. She asked me if I knew, but I didn't have any idea. I still don't for sure. I'm hoping it was Lori being missing and not because he had anything to do with it. I don't believe he could have hurt our little sister. He loved her."

"I understand, Jake. When you told me it was Tom who you'd seen in the park, I felt the same way. In the end, though, we need to find out who did it, no matter who it was. I'm not sure if you know this, but another girl was found dead in the park recently. The initial findings are similar to Lori's murder."

She heard Jake let out a deep breath. "Oh, my God, Aubrey. I hate to hear another girl died, but it does ease my mind about my brother being the killer. He's in Oregon and couldn't have done it. Right?"

"Well, yes. Jaime couldn't have killed this girl, for sure. But the detectives may want to get an alibi for him if we connect him to Lori's case." She scribbled some notes and paced the room. "I spoke with him yesterday. He sounded stoned when he answered my questions. Was he frequently smoking weed then, too?" She cringed at the bluntness of her question.

"He was, sad to say. He never seemed motivated after Lori died. His grades dropped, he lost interest in the Science Club. He loved that club, but he started smoking weed and cigarettes non-stop. He lost interest in everything."

"But he wasn't smoking before she was killed?"

"Not that I knew, and I think I would have. Her death hit him hard."

"Okay. I appreciate your help, Jake. How long will you be at this number?"

"I'll be here a week, then I'm off to Kenya. If you need to speak with me again, call the number I gave you for my office, and they'll let me know. I hope you solve Lori's murder, but I hope my brother didn't have anything to do with it."

"I understand. Enjoy your bush adventures. I know the photos will be fabulous."

"Thanks. Keep in touch."

****

Aubrey checked on Dan Hunter's address. After work, she drove to his home and rang the doorbell, her ID in hand.

Although older than his yearbook picture, she recognized him immediately. His angular face, dimples, and light blue eyes hadn't changed, so much as enhanced, his appearance. The adolescent pimples were gone, leaving flawless skin, strong cheekbones, and disheveled chocolate brown hair.

"Dan Hunter?" she asked, holding up her ID.

"Yes. Who are you?"

"I'm Officer Stanton. I'm working on a cold case where your name came up. I'd like to tie up some loose ends, and I'm hoping you can help me. Would now be a good time?"

"Um, sure, I guess. Come in." He shrugged his shoulder and opened the door wider.

"Thanks. Is there a place we can sit and talk?"

"Of course. In here."

She followed Dan to the living room, and they took seats across from each other. The room was a mix of bachelor pad garage sale items, and expensive, but worn, furnishings. Even with her untrained eye, she swore one tiny painting was an original Kandinsky, her favorite artist. The living room was clean and uncluttered. *He must dust pretty often. I have more than this on my table. Neat freak?*

"What cold case is this?" he asked, drawing her attention away from his decor.

"It's the Lori Harris murder from back in 1963. We have most of what we need, but there're a few loose ends. During the investigation, we came across a group of school friends you may know. I'm hoping you can help me close the case." Aubrey pulled out a notepad, her recorder, and flipped to a blank page. She turned on the recorder.

"Do you recall any of these names: Oliver Larson, Greg Wyatt, Jaime or Jake Harris, Tom Stanton, John Watson, or Peter Jackson?" She threw in a few extra names, so he wouldn't know who she was focusing on. She watched him closely for any indications of uneasiness or defensiveness, but he was charming and relaxed.

"Um, what's with the recorder?"

"I'm required to record all conversations I have about the case so they can be transcribed properly." She smiled at him. "It's not a problem, is it?"

"I guess not. Yeah. I knew Greg Wyatt, Tom Stanton, who I believe is your brother, Jaime and Jake Harris. I think Greg was friends with Oliver Larson, but I didn't know the others. I've never heard of Peter or John."

"Were you friends with any of them?" She made some notes, hoping he would respond more freely if she weren't staring at him.

"I hung around with Tom a little but none of the others."

"Are you still in touch with anyone from that group?"

"I saw Tom at your father's funeral. We talked a bit and caught up, but no, not really. I'm busy with school and working at my father's law firm."

"Tom went out the night of the funeral. Did he happen to meet up with you? He was staying at my place and came home late. I'm curious who he spent his time with." She smiled and sat back in the chair.

"We met and had a beer at the Pour House. I had to work the next day, so I didn't stay long. He's different than I remember, as I'm sure you know." She didn't. "But aren't we all?"

"I haven't spent any real time with him in a while. How do you think he's different?" She scratched her head and scrunched her eyes.

Is he trying to implicate Tom?

"I don't know. He seems ... darker, maybe. Troubled. I'm not sure. He said he's doing something with mining. At the time, I thought it was because he's alone so much. Perhaps I've forgotten how he used to be." He shook his head, looking at the floor.

When he looked up again, he wore an unnaturally bright smile. *What is he hiding?*

"Thank you for your time, Mr. Hunter. If there's anything else, I'll be in touch." She gathered her things and stood to leave.

"I hope I helped, although I don't know how. I hope you catch whoever did it."

He put his hand on the door to close it.

As Aubrey walked out of the house, she turned and asked, "Did you know Erin Grant, by any chance?"

She watched his eyes flash in anger, and his mouth harden.

"No, I didn't." He closed the door.

Gotcha!

Chapter 17

Aubrey raced home, threw her purse and papers on the table, and grabbed the phone to call Steve. Her hands shook with excitement as she dialed his number.

"Ohmygod, ohmygod, answer, please." She looked around the room for Kizzy. *She must be sleeping and didn't hear me come in. She's been sleeping a lot more lately. I'll go find her in a minute.*

When Rollins picked up the line, she blurted out her news. "Steve, I'm back from talking to Dan Hunter. I *know* he was involved, possibly in both murders. He — "

"Whoa! Hold on, Aubrey. Let me get something to write on and tell me everything. You recorded him, right?"

"Yes, of course. Great advice, by the way." She stood, waiting, and tapping her foot in an unheard rhythm.

"Okay, I got a notepad. What happened? Start at the beginning."

Aubrey relayed the conversation and Dan's reaction when she asked about Erin Grant.

"He tried to be charming and deferential but couldn't hold onto the charade when I asked about Erin. He admitted meeting with Tom the night she disappeared."

"I think you've got a lot of good stuff but nothing specific enough to request a warrant to search his house. It's a lot of supposition and intuition. Unfortunately, you need more. I don't mean to burst your bubble, but it's not enough. I *do* think you're right about him being involved, but it also includes your brother. Don't you want to be absolutely certain before charging headlong into this?"

She chewed her lip. "You're right. I was so excited to finally get somewhere."

"I understand, but you have to take this slowly. You've put all of these guys on notice. You have to watch your back now. You already have a harasser, for want of a better word.

You've been overtly threatened, more than once. Perhaps it's time to turn it over to a more seasoned detective?"

Aubrey sighed. "I know you're right, but they were so dismissive when I talked to them before. Why would they take me seriously now?" *I'll feel like I've failed Lori by not finishing it myself.*

"You've done a fantastic job getting this far, Aubrey. Don't sell yourself short. I'm sure Lori would be proud of what you've accomplished, but you're in over your head and could get yourself killed. If Dan's the killer, he could come after you. He's probably on the phone right now talking to your brother, or Greg Wyatt, or Jaime Harris, or whoever his partner is. Maybe he doesn't have a partner and will simply choose to silence you. You have to be careful, and you have to tell your sergeant. Give him a copy of your notes and make several copies of the recording you made today. Protect yourself and your investigation."

Aubrey paced the floor as she listened to her mentor's words. "Do you really think he would come after me? He seems to like helpless girls and women, not cops. After all, he knows I have a gun, and I know how to use it." She heard a small noise in the kitchen. *Oh, there's Kizzy. She was probably sleeping under the table.*

She heard him exhale. "You're not giving him enough credit. Listen to me. He's dangerous. We've only had two murders here, but it doesn't mean he hasn't committed more in other places … and gotten away with it. Aubrey, pay attention to me. Tell someone else: your sergeant, the detectives, a fellow cop you can rely on."

She stifled a laugh at the idea there was anyone in the department she could trust other than Sergeant Mills. *I wish I could trust the other guys.*

"You're right. I'll make copies of the tape right now and take them to the station, along with my notes. Thanks so much, Steve. You've been a great help."

She hung up the phone and looked for her recorder. *I must have left it in the car. That was stupid.* She headed for the front door, heard a noise behind her, then the world went black.

****

Aubrey woke with a violent headache. She blinked her eyes repeatedly before understanding dawned. She felt the roughness of a cloth hood over her head, the tape on her mouth pinched. Her throat constricted with fear as she struggled to breathe. Aubrey attempted to move only to discover her wrists and ankles were bound. She thrashed. *Where am I? Slow down, breathe, don't hyperventilate. Think!*

As the first wave of panic slowed, she concentrated on what was around her. She detected a rancid smell emanating from the lumpy mattress she rested on. *Blood? Something else ... feces, perhaps? Yuck, disgusting. Urine. There's more ... chemicals, bleach, and a gross stink. Ugh.* She struggled with her bindings, hoping to loosen them.

I must be alone, I don't hear anything. No, that's not right. I do hear ... what? Metal scraping? Something industrial. Where am I? How long have I been here?

Icy water splashed over her head, rivulets running down the back of her shirt. She gasped and heard laughing.

"Hey, bitch, didn't I tell you to drop the case or you'd regret it? Stupid cunt. I tried to warn you to stay away." He kicked her hard in the ribs.

Grunting at the unexpected assault, she caught her breath and placed the voice ... her mysterious caller, not Dan Hunter.

"Now, you be a good girl and stay put." He chuckled. "You couldn't move if you wanted to."

Aubrey listened to his receding footsteps. She waited until a door shut, and, confident he was gone, again attempted to release the tape holding her wrists. *I am so screwed here. I should've talked to the detectives sooner.*

She choked back tears, shook her head. *Crying won't get me out of this mess. Was Lori held here? What about Erin? Who is this shithead?* Her thoughts tumbled in all directions. *Is he going to kill me? Torture me? Rape me?*

After what seemed like hours of struggling, she felt a slight loosening of the restraint on her wrists. Relief flooded her body, and she relaxed. *Okay, take a breath, go at it again, it's working.*

"Hey, baby. How ya doing?" His body odor hit her before his fist did.

Tears welled in her eyes. Her face was on fire, and her nose gushed blood.

"Maybe we could play some games together before my boys arrive. I'd hate to have to share you. Even with a bag on your head, I can tell you're the passionate type. I'm not sure you'd be as much fun as your little friend, Lori. She didn't understand what I wanted from her, so she put up a good fight. I eventually got what I wanted, though. Nice and tight." He laughed, then kicked her in the back. "Now, Erin was a delight. She begged and pleaded as I raped her repeatedly. My boys did, too. We all had a great time. And I think you should know I have many interesting implements to make our time together memorable. Would you like me to tell you? No, I believe it will be better if you find out what I have planned gradually. Hmmm, I wonder how used you are? I guess we'll find out, won't we? But don't worry, you'll be plenty used up when we finish with you. I think we'll start tonight. Not that you'll care by then."

Terror engulfed her as she struggled to breathe. She blew the blood out of her nose to clear her airway as best she could, taking long, slow breaths. Never had she felt so helpless. *No one will miss me for at least twenty-four hours. Actually, I have no idea what day or time it is. What will they think happened to me? Oh, God, I could be dead by then.*

She pushed her despair aside and focused on the unknown man. With the hood over her head, she couldn't see him but was able to tell he'd walked farther away. His stench receded.

Is he leaving again? He's walking around. Leave. Leave. I can get out of here if I work hard enough at it. Her wrists stung, and she could feel seeping, sticky, wet blood.

The punch to her gut stole her breath. *Shit, that hurt. I should've paid more attention to where he was. Not that I could've prepared myself.* She fought the urge to vomit since her mouth was taped shut. Scared she would choke on it, she forced the bile down.

"That's what interfering bitches get when you meddle in business that's not your concern. Your questions have put my friends and me under the microscope, and I don't like being there. Your buddy, Rollins, should be getting a visitor about now. Maybe he'll join us in a bit. Then you two busybodies will get what you deserve." He laughed. "Maybe I'll let him watch the action with you later. And you can watch as we skin him."

Aubrey heard him clomping around the room, the sound echoing in the space. *Oh, Steve. What have I gotten us into? I'm so sorry.*

****

Steve Rollins finished his lunch and was in the middle of cleaning up when the doorbell rang. He looked through the peephole and saw a clean-cut young man standing on his porch with a clipboard in his hand. He debated answering it but opened the door a mere three inches.

As he glanced through the gap, the man charged through, knocking Steve off balance. His years of police training kicked in. He swung at the stranger. His fist tapped the guy's head, but it was an ineffectual glancing blow. The assailant advanced on him.

"What do you want? Who are you?" he shouted as he dodged a punch intended for his face.

Steve's kick connected with the intruder's knee, and he heard the man curse. He grabbed the man's shirt and felt the material tear, a button popped loose and struck his cheek. Steve blindsided him with an uppercut to the chin. Hard. The man fell over a side table to the floor, unconscious.

"Sonofabitch. Seems Aubrey stepped into a hornet's nest and brought me along. They must have seen her come here."

Steve rummaged in a junk drawer, located old handcuffs he'd kept around, secured the unconscious man, and called the police station.

"911. What's your emergency?"

"This is retired Detective Steve Rollins. I was attacked in my home. Transfer me to the detectives working on the recent Grant murder."

He rubbed his shoulder where the door had caught him when the guy busted in.

"Detective Weston."

"Hey, Hal. This is Steve Rollins."

"Hi, Steve. How ya doin'?"

"I'm fine, no thanks to this idiot handcuffed in my living room. He attacked me as I opened my door, and I believe it's related to Erin Grant's murder."

"Really? Why?"

"Too much for the phone. Get over here as fast as possible. Check if Officer Stanton is there. She's opened a can of worms, and I want to make sure she's okay. I haven't heard from her in over twenty-four hours. You remember where I live?"

"Yeah. I can do that. See you in twenty."

Chapter 18

Fifteen minutes passed before Detectives Weston and Brady arrived at Steve Rollins's house. The assailant, handcuffed in his living room, was still unconscious. Brady searched the man's pockets for identification and found his wallet. The driver's license showed his name as Jeffrey Phillips, twenty-eight years old, with an address in Mill's Creek, a nearby town.

Weston slapped Phillips's face, attempting to rouse him, but without success. He would need to be checked out at the hospital.

"I wish I knew what his intentions were," Rollins said. "He rammed through my door with a purpose, a not-very-nice purpose either. Is a patrolman coming to take him?" He scratched his head. "Was Aubrey at work today?"

"Yeah, they'll be here soon. She wasn't at the station, and her sergeant said she wasn't at roll call either, which is not like her. He claims she's never taken a sick day. What are you thinking, Steve?" asked Hal.

"I think as soon as they haul this piece of shit away, we need to go to her house and check on her. In fact, if one of you can stay with this guy, maybe we can go now." His brow furrowed. "I'm pretty worried about her."

"Brady can stay here. The ambulance is on its way. It shouldn't take long."

Steve motioned for Hal Weston to follow him out to his car. They left the detective's car for Brady, so he could meet them later.

"So, tell me what's been going on with Stanton that would cause all of this," Hal asked, getting into Steve's Buick.

"She's been investigating the Harris cold case. I thought you knew."

"Yeah, I guess I did. She stopped by the bureau one day and told us almost nothing, so I forgot about it. One other day, she called to talk about her harasser and phone calls she'd been getting. Talked to Brady, who blew her off, said he didn't have time for her problems. Now, I can see both may have been mistakes. Is there any chance these things are unrelated?"

"Well, sure. There's always a chance, but Aubrey told me the calls were threatening her about the investigation, so I don't believe so. And there must be a team, or at least partners involved. Aubrey thought Dan Hunter was involved, but she never mentioned this Jeff guy's name. Maybe she has more information at her house."

As they turned into Aubrey's driveway, Hal said, "Steve, look. Her car's here, but the front door isn't closed. Did you bring your weapon, by any chance?"

"No, I didn't think about it. Sorry."

"Here. Take my backup gun. I don't know what we'll find in there, and I'd feel better if we're both prepared for anything."

Steve checked the handgun Hal handed to him, saw it had a full magazine in it, and opened his car door. They approached the front of the house.

"Steve, go around back."

"Roger that." Steve jogged around the house, watching for anything out of place. At the back door, he found Aubrey's dog, Kizzy, whimpering on the grass with an obviously broken leg and bleeding from a cut on her head.

"Hey, girl. It's okay." He gave her a gentle pat, hoping to reassure her that she wasn't alone. "I'll take care of you in a minute. Hang in there."

He looked through the back door window, saw nothing, and tried the handle. It opened.

Gun held chest high, he entered through the back as he heard Hal coming through the front.

"Police! Show yourself! Police!" Hal shouted from the living room.

Together, they checked the house for intruders, found no one, but could see signs of an altercation at the front door. Blood speckled the entryway, and the phone had been knocked off the stand, papers scattered on the floor.

"She's been taken. The back door was open, her dog's in the backyard, and it looks like she has a broken leg. Let me get something to wrap her up while you call it in."

Steve walked around the blood spatters and pulled a towel from the linen closet. He overheard Hal calling for crime scene techs and went back outside to gather Kizzy. Aubrey's vet would take care of the dog and board her while they hunted for her mistress. He gently placed Kizzy in the passenger seat of his car and walked over to where Hal stood waiting.

"Hal, I think Aubrey's still alive. There wasn't enough blood there to indicate he'd killed her … yet. Besides, he likes to keep them for a day or two, so we still have time to find her. Brady should be here shortly. I'm going to take the dog to the vet's. I'll be back to figure out our next move."

"Yeah, I agree. I'll be here. I didn't notice any notebooks on our walkthrough, did you?"

"No, but I wasn't really looking."

He walked over to Aubrey's car, glanced in and saw the tape recorder on the passenger seat. He looked around to determine if anyone could see him and realized the detective was in the house. He strolled to the far side of the car, tried the door latch, and opened it. He reached in and, using his handkerchief to prevent his fingerprints on it, took the recorder, secreting it in his inside jacket pocket. Fortunately, it was one of the newer, smaller versions. He wiped the door latch to clear his fingerprints.

"I'll listen to this first, and if there's anything of value, I'll let them know I saw it in her car. Then they can officially retrieve it," he muttered under his breath.

Steve took Kizzy to the vet's office, which took longer than he'd hoped. The vet took Kizzy to an exam room while Rollins explained how and where he'd found her.

"I'll pay for whatever care she needs. You may have to keep her for a while, but I'll let you know."

"It's no problem," the doctor replied. "Kizzy is one of my favorites. She'll be safe and cared for here or, if need be, at my house. Go get whoever did this to her."

He looked at his watch, it had been thirty minutes since he'd left Aubrey's house. He had time to listen to the tape before the crime scene boys would be done. After he'd listened to the tape twice, he rewound it to the beginning. There was nothing on it that Aubrey hadn't already told him. He started his car. *I want to get back to her house before the crime scene guys leave.* Steve drove a little above the speed limit, but unfortunately, the techs were packing up as he arrived. He was anxious to go through the house again, but more thoroughly, with Hal.

Brady blocked his way, placing an arm across the doorway as Steve was about to enter. "Sorry, Rollins, you can't go in there. It's a crime scene, and you're no longer an active detective. You have to wait outside."

"I thought you'd go to the hospital with the asshole."

"Nah, we sent a uniform with him. I'll go see him later when he's awake."

Steve sighed. "Okay, I understand. But make sure you look for a notebook or pad, maybe in her purse, if it's in there. She told me on the phone she'd taped her conversation with Hunter, and she had notes on several conversations with other people who could be involved."

"Look, Rollins, we know you used to be good at this, but we know what we're doing. You had your chance to close the case. Stand back." Brady crooked a smug smile. "This is our baby now. Let us do our job."

He bit his lip at Brady's patronizing tone. He needed them if they were going to find Aubrey in time. Steve watched as Brady ducked under a strip of crime scene tape and entered the house. He strolled around to the far side of Aubrey's car and, holding the recorder with his handkerchief, placed it slightly under the front passenger seat. He returned to the other side to wait for the detectives to appear.

Hal exited the house twenty minutes later, shaking his head. "Nothing helpful in there to lead us where they may have taken her. No notes, other than the few papers we found on the floor, no recorder. With the small amount of blood near the front door, whoever it is must've knocked her out and took her out the back, so the neighbors wouldn't see anything."

"I wanted to wait until you were done in there, but I can see her recorder poking out under the passenger seat of her car. I'm surprised the crime scene guys didn't find it." He held his breath, hoping they hadn't looked.

"Since Stanton wasn't abducted from her car, we saw no reason to have them search it. Let me get some gloves and an evidence bag. We'll check it out at the station."

"So, what next? How are we going to find her?" Steve asked as Brady exited the house.

"*We're* not going to find her," Hal said, eyebrows raised. "Brady and I are. You need to go home, review everything she's told you, any notes you have on the investigation, any insights you can think of. Call me if you think of anything, but it's now in our hands. We'll do everything possible to find her. She *is* one of ours, and we want her back." Hal patted Steve's shoulder. "I'm glad she confided in you, so at least we know what to look for, but I wish she'd have told either her sergeant or us what she was doing."

"She tried to tell you, but you both brushed her off." Steve's voice betrayed his anger.

"Well, I remember her coming into the bureau but couldn't hear what was said. We were in the middle of trying to figure out who killed Erin Grant and didn't think the two were related. Who knew a rookie cop could get so far on her own. Of course, now we know she had your help."

"Not really. Aubrey did it on her own with very little advice from me. She's smart and determined, and you need to find her. I'll call you if I have any ideas or more information."

****

Steve returned to the vet's office to check on Kizzy and headed home. He pulled out his notebook and read and reread everything Aubrey'd shared with him. He also reread his copy of the original file on Lori Harris, looking for any clues as to where she may have been held during the time between her abduction and the discovery of her body in the park.

He reviewed the connections between the suspects Aubrey had spoken to, trying to find a link to any particular place they might have hung out in. Finally, he looked for addresses and phone numbers for each boy, now man, involved. He would call or visit them, with or without police authority. Since he no longer wore a badge, he wouldn't be hampered by legalities. Maybe he could get one of them to talk. It was personal now.

Steve called Greg Wyatt first. Since he had been Oliver's best friend, he seemed a likely first step.

"This is Greg."

"This is Steve Rollins. I'm a retired detective in Spencer, Michigan, and have been working with Officer Stanton on the

Lori Harris murder case. I understand you spoke with her recently."

"Yeah ... so what?"

"Officer Stanton has been abducted. We believe one of your old friends may have had a hand in it. Have you spoken to anyone regarding this case in the past few days?"

"No one out there. I live in California, ya know." Wyatt's snide response caught Steve's attention.

"Yes, I *do* know, and don't get smart with me. I know your connection to Oliver Larson, and he is still our prime suspect. Your best friend most likely kidnapped, tortured, and killed an eight-year-old girl, and I think you knew something about it, even if you didn't participate. I need to know where he hung out, favorite places, abandoned buildings, or warehouses, that sort of thing." He gave Greg a chance to respond, but there was none.

"It will go a long way toward helping you if the district attorney decides you were involved. Especially now, since he either had a partner who is still active or one of your other friends decided to step in as a copycat. I'm sure you know Erin Grant was murdered, and now a police officer is missing, taken from her home." He waited, holding his breath, hoping his bluff worked.

"Ollie's been dead a long time. I don't remember where he used to go. Besides, the city's changed. Some of the old places were torn down or bought out by new owners. Any place I tell you probably isn't the same now."

"I don't care. Tell me what you know. I'll put together the rest."

"Give me your number, and I'll call you back if I think of anything."

"We don't have time. Think fast, *now*. Whoever took Aubrey has threatened her in the past, and her life is in danger. We need a starting point to look for her. Should I visit your mother and tell her how you and your best friend Ollie spent your leisure time?"

"Hey, now. Don't get my mother involved in this. She's had a hard life and doesn't need any grief from you. Give me a second."

Steve waited for Greg's conscience to overcome his loyalty.

A couple minutes passed before Greg spoke again. "Okay. There was one place where Ollie and I hung out. It's an old tire surplus shop, hardly ever used. They store old tires in it until they have enough to haul them to the dump. It's behind the Morgan Cold Storage building on Jackson Street. I don't know if it's still there, but I always found the place creepy. I hope you find her." He hung up.

Steve grabbed a phone book and searched for the building Wyatt had mentioned. A cold storage building would be a perfect place to hide a body until the killer or killers were ready to display it somewhere. The company appeared to be out of business, but he knew where Jackson Street was.

"Oh, shit, I forgot to give Hal his gun back. I hope I won't need it. I'll go check it out, and if there seems to be anything to this, I'll call Hal to come look," he muttered to himself, as he located his keys and ran for his car. "Aubrey, hang in there. I'm coming for you."

Chapter 19

Aubrey struggled against her restraints. She'd managed to loosen the tape on her wrist but couldn't get her hands through the opening. She'd succumbed to a full bladder and knew she stunk of urine but had no choice. She stopped struggling when she heard the door open, laid still, feigning sleep. *Please don't hit me again. I'm so hungry, tired, and sore. I don't know how much longer I can hold on.*

"What the hell is wrong with you? Why would you bring her here?" She recognized Dan Hunter's voice echo through the mostly empty, large space. "God, it stinks in here."

"She wouldn't quit. I called her a few times, even put that damn possum on her back door like you suggested, but she kept asking questions. What did you say to her when she was at your house? You must have given her something, or she wouldn't still be investigating," her assailant and captor shouted at Hunter.

"You're an idiot, Larson. Don't you think the cops are going to know she spoke with me before you snatched her?"

Larson? I thought he was dead? What are they going to do with me? She silently pleaded, *Please, someone find me.*

"Listen, Dan. I didn't have to bring you into my little enterprise. It was because you knew my baby brother that you were included. Your fun and games with that Grant bitch is the only reason I've let you continue to be a part of this."

Ohhh, Oliver was the baby brother. Stupid of me not to look for older brothers instead of only younger ones. Now what? Poor Erin.

"Has she seen your face?" Hunter asked.

"No, of course not. I'm the one who's done this a million times, not you. Who are you to question me, asshole?" Aubrey could hear Larson stomping around.

"Because I know the law, and I'm trying to keep us from going to jail. Where the hell is Jeff, anyway? I thought you sent him to get that old detective, Rollins."

"Hell, I don't know. He should be back by now. Maybe there was a glitch."

"A glitch?" Hunter's tone changed to a menacing growl. "Rollins is a fucking detective. Do you suppose he outsmarted or even managed to catch him? Jeff's probably on the way to the police station right now, ready to spill his guts."

"No, he's not. Jeff's been a great gofer, and no one suspects him. I've intentionally kept him out of sight since he approached me about my little games last year. I think you know how excited he is to be part of our plans. Jeff wouldn't let himself get caught. If he did, he knows the consequences; gives him an incentive to keep his mouth shut." Larson balanced his wickedly sharp skinning knife on his thumb.

"Maybe Rollins wasn't home, and he's waiting for him to show up. Besides, no one knows about this place. They can't find us here." Larson threw the knife at a board propped against the wall, expertly sticking the tip into the soft wood.

"Really? Ollie used to bring his boy, Greg, here on occasion. If they get to him, we're in big trouble. I think we should dump her somewhere and forget about Rollins."

"What's the matter, Danny-boy? Getting cold feet on me? Greg is out in Cali, he's no use to them," Larson taunted. "I'm not dumping her until I've amused myself with her. A few more calculated kicks and she'll be so complacent, we can do anything we want to her. You can leave and wash your hands of this. I'll enjoy her by myself or with Jeff when he shows up. Now, there's a guy who knows how to have a good time and can be quite creative."

Aubrey attempted to pull her hand through the tape without alerting them. *I have to get free enough to defend myself here.* She could feel sweat beads on her forehead and her heart pounding. With her blood slathering her skin, she released her left hand from the binding. *Ohmygod, I got it.* Trying to remain inconspicuous, she lay still, hoping to hear more.

"You're a real bastard, aren't you?" Hunter replied.

"Don't you call me a bastard, asshole!" Larson shouted.

"Oomph. You hit me!" Dan roared.

Aubrey heard scuffling and exclamations. *I hope Hunter comes out on top. Maybe I can negotiate with him.* She heard the door open, someone leave and slam it shut.

"Well, well, well. What have we got here? I see you've managed to get your hands loose. I guess I'll have to fix that," said Larson, and kicked her in the kidney.

She groaned in agony as he grabbed her arm and yanked her onto her stomach, forced her arms together behind her, and retaped her from her wrists to her elbows. Pain shot up her arms to her shoulders, and a stabbing pain in her back made every movement torture. She breathed carefully through her partially blocked broken nose.

"Let's see you get out now, bitch. But don't fall asleep, I'll be back shortly to begin showing you how real men treat their women." Larson laughed and walked away.

Aubrey stayed on her stomach, shivering from the pain and her fear. She waited until she heard him leave. Writhing on the lumpy mattress, she increased her efforts to free her legs. She rolled halfway over, trying to get more leverage and growled through the tape with her frustration. *It's no good. They're too tight. I'm gonna die here. Maybe I can crawl out of here.*

Thrashing on the filthy bedding, she didn't hear the door slide open. When she felt someone touch her shoulder, she jerked away. Expecting another punch or kick, she wriggled across the mattress. Kicking out blindly, she struck something. *Take that, asshole!* Through her panic, she felt emboldened to try again. She lashed out again and again until the person caught her legs.

"Aubrey, it's Steve, it's Steve. Let's get you out of here. Ouch, you got me good with the first kick."

"Mmmph?" *Oh, God, thank you.*

He pulled off her head covering, gently removing the tape over her mouth. He barely managed to conceal his concern when he saw the blood, bruises, and broken nose. He pulled out a pocket knife and cut her bindings at her wrists and ankles.

She tried to stand, her knees giving out with the effort.

Steve grabbed her under the arms and lifted her. "Here, let me help you up. They might come back. We need to hurry."

Aubrey couldn't respond as she sobbed, gulping breaths, now that she could breathe through her mouth, and clung to his shoulders. She pulled herself together enough to croak, "Let's go."

Steve carried her so he could move faster. Inching around the door, they moved away from the warehouse and down the street to his car. She moaned with every step.

"I'm so embarrassed, I wet myself in there, and I know I stink. I don't want to mess up your car."

"Don't worry about it. I have a blanket I'll put down. I'm taking you to the hospital. I'll call Hal Weston once we get there. I have some water in my thermos if you want it. Don't drink too much, I don't know what damage he's done to you. Take sips."

She reached for the bottle, battling the numbness in her hands, and forced herself not to chug the liquid down her parched throat. Sip by sip the rawness alleviated.

"I didn't realize how thirsty I was until I took the first drink."

****

As they approached the hospital, Aubrey asked, "How did you find me? How did you even know I was gone?"

"A guy broke into my house and attacked me. After I secured him, I called the station and had Weston check on whether you'd shown up for work. When he said you hadn't, we went to your house and saw some blood and the phone stand knocked over. Your doors weren't locked. He hurt Kizzy, but she's at the vet's and should be fine." He glanced at Aubrey and saw her face drain of color.

"I called Greg Wyatt, and he told me this was a favorite haunt of Oliver Larson's, back in the day. Luckily, someone was still using it. I'm so glad I found you. Do you know who took you?"

"What did he do to Kizzy?" Aubrey imagining the worst for her little dog, and tears fell down her cheek. *I'll kill him if I have to put her to sleep because of her injuries.*

"Her leg is broken, and she had a cut on her head, but she's going to be fine. Your vet has her."

"Oh, my poor baby. Thanks for taking care of her." She swiped away her tears. "In answer to your question, yes, Oliver's older brother abducted me. I don't know his name. Dan Hunter was there before you showed up. They fought over Larson taking me."

She suppressed a groan when he hit a small bump in the road as he raced across town. She sat curled on the bench seat, holding her stomach and sipping more water.

"We'll be there in a minute. I need to get Brady and Weston over to the warehouse. Maybe he'll come back."

"I agree. We have to catch these guys. So, there's at least three of them involved?"

"Sounds like it. We'll get 'em. We have Jeff Phillips already, the guy at my house, handcuffed to his hospital bed."

****

Steve pulled into the emergency room dropoff and turned off the car. He grabbed an empty wheelchair and pushed it to the passenger side. Aubrey slumped into it, and he wheeled her inside. After the nurse took her to an exam room, Steve called Hal Weston at the station.

"Hal, I found Aubrey. I brought her to the ER. It looks like she's been badly beaten. Can you send a patrolman to guard her door here? I don't want the bad guys to discover her missing and come looking for her."

"That's great you found her. Where? Who grabbed her? Never mind, I'll get a patrolman there pronto, and I'll be there as fast as I can. I'll bring Brady with me."

"No. Go to the warehouse across from the cold storage building on Jackson. That's where she was. It's a crime scene now. The guy may return there soon, and you could catch him before he has a chance to clean the place up. He's Oliver Larson's older brother. Oliver was the original suspect. Dan Hunter, the attorney's kid, is also involved. Come here once you get him."

The cop assigned to Aubrey's room arrived, taking a position outside her door.

Steve told the young officer, "Don't let anyone be alone with her. Not even a doctor or nurse. Make sure there are at least two people in the room. She can't defend herself, so it's up to you to protect her. Got it?"

"Yes, sir."

Steve paced the floor, waiting for someone to give him an update on Aubrey's condition. He watched people in distress, scared or hurt, stream by him; doctors and nurses running, walking and talking, or shouting orders as patients and visitors came and went. Nearly an hour passed before a doctor emerged.

"Are you family?" he asked Steve.

"Yes. I'm Aubrey's uncle," he lied. They wouldn't tell him anything if he wasn't related. "I brought her in. How is she?"

"She's pretty beat up. She has lacerations, a broken nose, maybe internal damage, but we're taking her to have a CT scan done. We installed the new technology last month, and its innovation will be a big help in seeing any damage. We'll know more once we have that. Overall, she's lucky. It looks like someone knew what he was doing. The kidney is our main concern. I'll update you as soon as I know more."

Steve took a deep breath and let it out slowly. He had to call her mother and wasn't looking forward to it. He saw pay phones next to several vending machines lining the hallway near the hospital lobby.

"This is Jayne," a cheery voice greeted him. He groaned, knowing it wouldn't be happy after he shared his news.

"Mrs. Stanton, this is Steve Rollins. I was the detect…"

"I know who you are," she interrupted him, her tone changing to a growl. "What do you want now? I thought I told you years ago to leave us alone."

"Yes, ma'am, I know. I'm calling to tell you that Aubrey is in the hospital. She's pretty beat up. Can you come now? I need to fill you in on a few things. I'll wait in the lobby."

She sighed. "I'll be there shortly." The shift to nonchalance stunned him.

****

It was a ten-minute drive from Jayne's house. She arrived forty-five minutes later, stage-walked into the lobby like she was a homecoming queen.

Steve had trouble keeping his expression neutral, not understanding a mother who wouldn't rush to her daughter's side, knowing she was injured. "Mrs. Stanton, did you have trouble getting here?"

"No. Why would you ask such a thing?" She scowled at him and scanned the lobby.

"I'm sorry. I thought you'd be here sooner, is all." He turned away so she wouldn't see his teeth grinding in anger.

"Well, I was taking a nap when you called. You didn't say it was urgent. I needed to fix my makeup and hair and change my clothes. I couldn't come here looking like a fishwife." Jayne glared.

"Of course. I apologize." He narrowed his eyes as he looked away from her. "Let's sit over here, and I'll tell you what happened. Would you like some coffee?"

"Thank you, yes. Cream and sugar, please." She looked with disdain at the orange plastic chair and sat primly on the edge, her purse perched on her lap.

Steve returned with coffee for both of them. "Aubrey was working on the Lori Harris case. Are you aware of this?"

Jayne took a sip of her coffee and grimaced. "Ugh, what is this swill?" She set her cup on the table. "Yes, I am. Aubrey accused her brother of killing the girl. I was irate with her." She frowned at Steve.

"I understand. She shared with me some of what she'd found. She must've hit a sore spot with someone she was investigating. I believe Aubrey was abducted by one of the suspects. She'd been receiving threatening phone calls, and on the way here, she claimed it was that man who took her." He hesitated to check her reaction. She was looking around the room. For a moment, he wasn't sure she was even listening to him.

"The doctors are doing some sort of scan now to determine the extent of her injuries. He beat her up while he had her. I'm telling you this so you won't be surprised when you see her."

"*You* were helping her? Is that why she's in this *mess*?" Jayne asked, eyes blazing.

"Aubrey came to me for help. She was determined to find Lori's killer and needed help to guide her. I told her to turn over what she'd found to a seasoned detective. She was about to do that when she was kidnapped."

"Is she going to be all right?" Jayne asked as though she were mentioning it was going to rain later.

Steve tried to hide his surprise at her matter-of-fact tone. "I believe so, unless they find something worse on the scan. Would you like me to call Tom for you?" His voice struggled to keep a polite tone.

Jayne stared at Rollins. "There's no need for that. We don't know anything yet. Why would I bother him at work to tell him nothing, basically?" She huffed and resettled her purse on her lap. An attractive doctor walked by, catching her eye and smiling. Jayne blushed and batted her eyelashes.

Steve shook his head and bit his lip at her response. "Okay. If you change your mind, I'd be happy to make the call for you."

"I can't imagine why I would need *you* to call my son. When I have more information, I'll speak to him. Thank you for the offer, but it's not necessary. After all, she's not dead, right?" She pulled out an emory board and began filing her nails.

Steve nodded, but his jaw tightened, and his hands clenched into fists.

Chapter 20

Conversation stalled as Aubrey's mother and Steve sat in the waiting room and drank coffee, watched people come and go. Thirty minutes earlier, the doctor had approached and told them, "Aubrey is being settled in her room. I need to hear from the radiologist before I can be certain her kidney isn't damaged by the assault. It shouldn't be much longer before you can see her."

Weston and Brady appeared a few minutes later. Steve introduced them to Jayne. "Excuse me, Mrs. Stanton, but I need to speak with the detectives for a moment," he said.

She waggled her fingers at them and resumed her makeup check in her compact mirror.

Weston suggested they move to a more private area. "I don't want Stanton's mother to overhear things before we know what happened," Weston said. "She doesn't seem very concerned, does she?"

Steve shrugged. "No, but people react in lots of different ways in a crisis." He knew how things worked. They walked to the far side of the room and stood by the large, fake Schefflera plants clustered there.

"How is she?" asked Brady. "The warehouse was a mess. The mattress on the floor had bloodstains, old and new, on it. And it stunk in there. We walked around and found some tools with blood also. I hope they weren't used on Stanton." He grimaced.

Steve filled them in on her condition. "I don't think so. Aubrey's been beaten in the face. Her nose is broken. She told me they kicked her in the ribs and kidney, so I'm hoping there's no internal damage. Still waiting for the doctor to verify. She was conscious when I found her but in rough shape. She told me he hadn't raped her but threatened to do it."

Weston scowled. "How exactly *did* you find her? I told you to lay off, and we'd handle this case." He shook his head and sighed. "I'm happy you located her, don't get me wrong, but what if they'd been there with her and killed you, too?"

"When I arrived, I saw a couple cars out front. I snuck up to the door and could hear two people arguing, so I hid behind some bushes until they left. I have done this a few times, you know." Steve narrowed his eyes at the other two. "What happened when you got to the warehouse?"

"No one was there. We sealed it and posted a few guys to guard it. And you haven't explained how you found her there." He lowered his voice, "Also, you still have my backup gun. If you have it with you, give it to me."

"Oh, sure. Sorry. It felt so natural, I forgot I had it." A sheepish grin played on Steve's face as he handed the weapon to Weston. "I reviewed the information Aubrey shared with me," he continued. "I noticed Oliver Larson and Greg Wyatt were best friends, so I called Greg. After some initial hesitation on his part, and some coaxing on mine, he told me the warehouse was a favorite hangout of Larson's. I thought I'd check it out, and if I found anything, I'd call you. When I got there, I heard arguing, and one of them say they should dump Aubrey and wash their hands of it. The other guy said he wasn't done with her yet. I knew there wasn't time for me to contact you before getting her out of there. Now you know who's involved, and you can chase them down."

Brady grumbled. "You should have called us to check out the place, not gone yourself. For chrissake, you know better than to play cowboy with something this big. We might've caught them."

"Honestly, would you have dropped everything and gone ... right then?" Steve cocked his head, raised his eyebrows.

"Yeah, probably ... maybe. We were in the middle of something when you called, so it might not have been immediately," Weston conceded. "But if you'd —"

"You know you wouldn't have. She might be dead right now, or being raped or tortured if I had waited around for you to go look," Steve interrupted him. "It's not like I don't know how to surveil someone. I went to see if it was worth your time, or if

Wyatt was leading me on a wild goose chase. I'd do the same again, in this situation."

Before Weston responded, the doctor appeared. The detectives and Steve joined Jayne to hear the news about Aubrey's condition.

"Hello, detectives, Mrs. Stanton," the doctor greeted them. "Aubrey's left kidney and several ribs are bruised. She's lucky none of her ribs are broken. We've set her nose, and, in time, she should be fine. You can see her now but only two at a time."

Jayne stood up. "Thank you, Doctor. Gentlemen, I'll go see my daughter alone now."

Detective Weston stepped forward. "Ma'am, we actually need to see her first. We need to document what she remembers before anyone else talks to her. We'll be as fast as we can, but you'll have to wait until we're done. I'm sorry."

Jayne sniffed and returned to her chair, pouting and clearly not happy about the detective's mandate. Steve joined her, sitting two chairs away, knowing conversation would be impossible, given her mood and dislike of him.

Weston and Brady walked toward the room the doctor indicated. The room was hospital stark. Various beeps sounded from the machines standing near the head of the bed. Brady crinkled his nose at the antiseptic smell permeating the space. Aubrey was propped up on pillows and dozing.

An IV line snaked out of her blanket up to a metal stand holding bags of antibiotics, saline, and a yellow liquid. White gauze secured and covered her broken nose. Its starkness contrasting with the multitude of purples, blues, and greens painting most of her face. She sported two swollen, black eyes; sporadic crusted blood the nurses hadn't cleaned yet, speckled her skin from hairline to neck, her lip was split. Bruises tattooed her arms where Larson had grabbed her when he taped her wrists together.

When Weston moved a chair closer to the bed, Aubrey startled from sleep. Screaming, she struggled to escape her hospital bed, but the bed rails prevented her from clambering over the top. Fear etched her bloodshot eyes, and tears escaped around the bandages.

"Aubrey ... Aubrey, calm down. You're safe here. We're Detectives Brady and Weston. Don't you recognize us?" Weston attempted to reassure her.

As he reached over to touch her arm, Jayne, Steve, and the patrolman guarding the door burst in. The cop stood back, surveyed the scene, and stepped outside the room.

"What are you doing to my daughter?" Jayne shrieked at the detective, grabbing his arm to yank him away. She looked at Aubrey and gasped, covering her mouth and stepping backward.

"Oh, my God." Her eyes looked at her daughter in horror.

Steve hurried to Aubrey's bedside to reassure her. "It's okay. I'm here with you."

"Steve, wa ... wasss goin' on?" Aubrey asked, her words sluggish and muddled. She latched onto his arm, her eyes wide and darting around at the people in her room. *Who are these people?*

Brady and Weston backed off. Jayne stood opposite the detectives, fidgeted, eyes lowered, and waited for Aubrey to calm.

A nurse ran in, looked around. She pointed to the detectives and Steve, and barked commands, "You, you, and you … out. She needs to rest. Out. Now." Her eyes bore into each man, and her finger pointed toward the door.

Aubrey motioned to her water glass, took a few sips, exhaled, and shook her head. "No, no, no. Sorry I screamed. I need Steve to stay. Mom?" Her voice grew stronger. Jayne nodded at her daughter. "Can you come back later? I need to talk to Steve."

Jayne huffed out the door. Brady left, as well. Weston didn't move.

"You know I can't leave you here with her alone, right, Steve?"

The nurse intervened. "Fine. You can stay." She nodded toward Weston. "Take a seat. Don't touch her, and if she starts to tire, you have to leave, too. Detective Rollins, you can stay because Ms. Stanton wants you here, and I think it'll be good to have someone she trusts with her right now. She's been given a heavy sedative. So, not too long. Got it?"

"Yes, Nurse Jenkins." He bent his head slightly in acknowledgment, stifling a smile.

Jenkins left, a frown on her face.

"So, you're 'Detective Rollins,' and I'm an interloper?" Weston asked, eyebrows raised.

"Jonnie Jenkins … JJ… and I go way back. She's a terrific nurse but strict about visitors." He turned his attention to Aubrey. "How you feeling, kid?"

"Like I got caught inside a cement mixer and poured out. I hurt everywhere. Did I thank you for rescuing me? I can never repay you." Unspilt tears formed again. "I can't stop crying. I think it was the water you gave me on the way over here." She and Steve chuckled. "Oh, that was a mistake. It hurts when I laugh."

"Aubrey, you thanked me plenty. You know you have to talk to Hal and tell him what you heard."

"Yeah, I know. It's fine." She looked toward Weston. "Sorry, Detective. I was half asleep when you came in and dreaming about what had happened. I thought you were Larson. I overreacted, I guess."

She gave him a weak smile as the tears fell down her bruised cheeks. *I hate feeling like a victim in front of these guys. I wish I could stop crying about everything. I thought I was stronger than this.*

"I'm sorry I scared you, Aubrey," Weston said, his tone gentle. "Can you answer some questions so we can catch the people who did this to you?"

She nodded.

"I don't want them to get away this time," Weston said. "Tell me everything you remember, and if you get too tired, let me know. Steve will stay here with us. But he can't say anything. He'll give his own statement later. Okay?"

"Yes, let's get them." She recounted as much as she remembered.

Weston took notes, while Steve held her trembling hand on the other side of the bed.

After half an hour, Aubrey's eyelids drooped. Her face showed signs of strain.

"You look tired, Aubrey." Steve turned to Weston. "I think you're done for now, Hal."

"Yeah, I agree. I'll go get Brady and see if we can find these assholes. Take care, Aubrey. I'll need to speak to you again, but get some rest."

Aubrey didn't respond as she fell into a deep sleep.

****

Jayne Stanton returned home after seeing Aubrey in the hospital. She sat on the edge of her bed and let her tears fall. She'd been stunned and revolted by Aubrey's injuries. "Why did

Aubrey decide to go into such a dangerous profession?" she said to the empty room. "I thought once I was divorced, things would get better. I feel so all alone. Aubrey hates me, and Tom lives so far away. Nothing goes right for me."

Her thoughts returned to her childhood. "I was happy living on the farm, wasn't I? I couldn't wait to leave, actually. We lived so far out in the country, there was nothing to do except chores. Hmmm, when have I been happy, truly happy? Before I got married, living with my sister in the city." She smiled at the memory. "Maybe for the first few years after John and I were married.

When I got pregnant with Tom, John changed. He'd never said he didn't want kids, but it was clear to me he didn't. We never even talked about it. I assumed he'd want them, especially a boy. He worked hard, long hours, but he wasn't happy. Then when Aubrey came along, Tom turned into a hellion and made things worse."

She sighed. "I can't change the past, and now I have to go back to the hospital. That's what good mothers do, but I don't want to, and I'm not sure Aubrey wants me there. She seems to have latched onto Rollins." She furrowed her brow. "I can't imagine why. What's so special about him?"

Jayne stood up, determined to put a bright face on and move through the day. Her boyfriend, Paul, had broken up with her, telling her he wasn't comfortable with Aubrey being a police officer, and that somehow, Jayne should have stopped her from going to the academy. The idiot claimed to be disappointed with her lack of parenting skills. "As if he would know. He's not a parent," she grumbled.

She glanced around the room. "I think I'll go shopping at the new mall. That always cheers me up." She fixed her makeup and grabbed her purse, anxious to get away from her gloomy thoughts.

****

Steve followed the detectives back to the station so he could write out his statement. Anxiety about leaving Aubrey unsettled his thoughts.

"I'm sure she'll be fine. After all, there's a patrolman standing, well, sitting outside her door," he murmured to himself as he drove. "The idiots who took her wouldn't try to get her again, not at the hospital, I hope."

He pulled into the parking lot and walked inside the station.

"I'm here to see Detective Weston," he told the young cop at the front, watched him call the detective's bureau, and took a seat.

"Sir, you can go up. Do you know where the bureau is located?"

He doesn't know who I am. Boy, do I feel really old right now. "Yes, I used to work there." He smiled as he watched the surprised expression on the man's face.

Steve climbed the stairs and stepped into the office. *Nothing changes around here, not even the vomit green paint on the walls.* The bustle of activity comforted, as a wave of nostalgia washed over him. *Good to see they're busy. I miss it more than I like to admit. But I don't miss the long hours.*

"Hey, Steve, come on over here," Weston called from the back of the room, waving to him.

"We're going into the interview room so you can write out your statement where it's quieter," added Brady.

"Okay, great. The sooner you catch these guys, the better. What are you doing to find them?" Steve asked.

Brady sighed. "You know I can't share that information with you. Trust me, we're working on it. Thanks to you and Aubrey, we know who we're looking for. I'm pretty sure when Larson returned to the warehouse and saw the cops all over it, he hightailed it out of town. We'll get him."

"You better, or Aubrey will never sleep well again … and neither will I."

Brady nodded and handed Steve a legal pad to write out the details he could provide. After he finished his statement, Steve returned to the hospital. His cop's intuition kept yelling at him to get back there. Something nagged at him, and he wasn't comfortable leaving her there alone.

****

Steve stopped at the gift shop to pick up some flowers for Aubrey. As he was walking toward her room, he saw the officer tasked with guarding her was gone. Steve rushed to her room and overheard shouting.

"Get out of here!" Aubrey yelled. Steve heard muffled sounds and ran into the room. The officer was struggling with her, and her IV line had been yanked out.

He threw the flowers on a chair, grabbed the cop, punched him, and tossed him to the floor. As the patrolman attempted to get up, Steve pointed and said, "Stay down there, shithead, or I'll make you wish you had."

Steve glanced at Aubrey. "Are you all right? What's going on here?"

"He came in, and I saw it was Scott Fuller. Remember I told you he hates me? I was afraid and told him to leave. He ignored me and stood by my bed, telling me how stupid I was for investigating the case." She narrowed her eyes, fought back tears, and said, "He grabbed my arm, and the IV pulled out. I was struggling with him when you arrived. He told me he wished I'd died since I didn't belong on the police force."

"Really? I'll tell you who doesn't belong in this police department is you, Fuller. Aubrey solved a cold case and discovered the identity of two serial killers and an accomplice. I think you're done here. I'll speak with your sergeant and request a new officer, one worth the title." He barely controlled his anger. *Aubrey's been though enough without this dickhead adding his two cents.* "Get out of here."

Fuller stood up, brushed off his uniform, and turned to Aubrey. "You haven't heard the last from me. Women shouldn't be cops, and I'll do everything I can to have you gone."

"Sorry, asshole, but I'm here to stay, even if you aren't." Lips pressed together, she pointed to the door.

"I guess we'll see." Fuller smirked at Aubrey and stormed out of the room. Muttering to himself, "How does she keep getting rescued? I have to find a way to force her out." He left the hospital.

After the door closed behind Fuller, Nurse Jenkins pushed into the room, saw the IV line pulled out, and Aubrey holding her hand over her arm to staunch the bleeding. She shook her head. "I heard yelling. Is everything okay? Never a dull moment with you here, is there?" Both women grinned as she reinserted the IV. "I'll be back to change the sheets since there's blood all over them now." She left Aubrey and Steve alone.

Steve picked up the flowers, now bedraggled and broken. "I brought you flowers to brighten your room. Sorry, they don't look so hot now." He placed them in her water pitcher.

"Thanks, Steve. They're beautiful." She smiled at him.

Steve used Aubrey's room phone to call the station and report Fuller's behavior and request the replacement guard. After speaking with Sergeant Mills and Detective Weston, he settled into a chair.

"Once again, you've come to my rescue. I don't know what he was planning, but I'm glad you arrived when you did. Can you check on Kizzy once the new cop shows up?"

"Of course, I can. I was thinking about what happens when you get released from here. I don't think it's safe for you to go home yet. You and Kizzy will need not only help but also protection. How about if you both come stay with me until this is over, and you're back on your feet?"

She frowned. "Are you sure? It could be a lot of work with Kizzy in a cast and me stumbling about."

Steve chuckled. "Yes, I'm sure. I have an extra bedroom and not much to do, so I'd be happy to take care of you both. I'll talk to the doctor before I leave and ask when he thinks you'll be ready to leave. Relax, I'll stay for a while. Get some rest, you look tired."

As Aubrey dozed off, Steve silently reviewed his next steps. *This isn't over yet.*

Chapter 21

Aubrey remained in the hospital for two more days, allowing her body and mind to heal. Steve visited every day, talking to her and letting her vent, cry, and remember. Get well cards appeared on her wall, and a variety of plants and colorful flowers surrounded the room.

The second afternoon, Steve told her, "I'm amazed by everything you've done, Aubrey. With a mother like yours, no disrespect intended, but she does seem distant and unconcerned for you, some people might have become submissive and eager to please. Instead, you've shown strength, intelligence, and courage. How did you manage it?"

Aubrey blushed through her bruises and shared with him her story of how she became so resilient.

"The winter before I found Lori, Tom took me across Main Street to play in a field. We had gotten a foot of snow the night before. I remember the temperature was colder than usual, and the sun's glare blinded me. We walked through the tall, dry grass where the wind had blown the snow away, and we slipped and slid on patches of ice. We ran into Tom's friends. On a bare spot in the open field, they'd built a fire to stay warm. Twelve-year-old boys didn't have much use for me, an eight-year-old girl, and they wouldn't let me near enough to the flames to keep away the cold."

She sipped her water, cleared her throat, and continued, "I complained and told him I wanted to go home. I was freezing. But he didn't listen. He teased me and said if I wanted to go, go. I went. I walked to Main Street, which was busy that day, and I remember being afraid to cross it. But I was determined to get home, so I waited for a break and ran across the road. When I arrived home, my fingers and toes were almost frostbitten.

"God, I can almost feel how cold I was, even now." She shivered. "I hate the winters and have since that day. The most troubling part of the incident, though, was my mother's reaction. She yelled at me, telling me how stupid I was, and asked where Tom was. I told her he was with friends. She dragged me into the car and berated me the entire time we looked for Tom. Never once did she express concern about how cold I was, much less allow a smidgen of praise for my decision to come home alone."

Aubrey gritted her teeth and drank more water, composing herself after revisiting the hurtful memory. "I decided that day I wouldn't depend on other people to take care of me. I think it's served me well so far, but I can also see the downside of a solitary life. We all need friends and people we can trust and rely on. You've shown me that side, Steve. I will always be grateful to you."

He smiled and gave her a gentle hug. "I promise to be there for you, Aubrey. You're like the daughter I never had. I know how brave and smart you are. I told you the first time I met you."

He stood and walked around the tiny room. He glanced at the good wishes taped to the green walls, looked out the window to hide his emotions, and covertly wiped his eyes. He turned and sat down on the edge of her bed.

"I knew you would do great things someday. Now, look at you. You've solved a fourteen-year-old murder and possibly many more, besides. You did what I couldn't, what no one else could. Don't ever question yourself about whether you're courageous, or if you're making the right decisions. You've got a good head on your shoulders, and you use it. Once you're back to work, I have no doubt you'll make an excellent detective. And you can always count on me to have your back and listen to you. Got it?"

Aubrey smiled through her tears. "Got it. Stop making me cry, my nose gets all stuffed up where it's still swollen."

****

Aubrey's mother appeared late the next morning at the hospital.

Strolling into Aubrey's room, dressed to the nines, she greeted her daughter, "Good morning, darling. That policeman outside your door questioned me about coming into your room. He made me show ID. How impertinent of him. Anyway, so sorry I didn't make it here yesterday. How are you feeling?" Rather than look at Aubrey, her eyes scanned the room full of flowers and cards. She pursed her lips. "I see you've gotten plenty of attention from friends and co-workers. I'm not sure how getting kidnapped and beaten up deserves that."

"I didn't do it intentionally, you know. I was doing my job. It's nice to know people care about me. I'm doing better, thanks for asking. The cop at the door's doing what he was told to do. Sorry if it was a problem. I know you're busy, you don't have to come here. The doctor says I'll be getting out soon."

"Well, of course, I would come to see you. Don't be silly. I don't really like hospitals, though. Ever since my father, your grampa, was in the sanitorium, I've been uncomfortable in them."

"Grampa was in a sanitorium? Why?" *Mom sharing with me? That's new.*

"Oh, honey, I'm sure I told you about that. Daddy caught tuberculosis in Alaska, working on the pipeline, and they sent him home to recuperate. It was awful. The place was dingy and smelled so horrible, a bit like here." She wrinkled her nose, held a handkerchief under it. "I hated going to visit him." She looked around and found a chair, pulled it a fraction closer to the bed.

"The doctors released him to attend my wedding to your father, but he had so many restrictions. We had to wash all his dishes and silverware separately. He had to have his own room to sleep in, and his bedding had to be sterilized in hot bleach water. It was a lot of work keeping him comfortable, and being careful not to catch it ourselves." She sighed. "Anyway, that's why I don't like to come here. I'm glad you'll be getting out soon."

"Gosh, Mom, I didn't know that. But he got well again, right?"

"Oh, yes, of course, he did." Jayne sniffed and stood. "I have a lunch date, so I need to go. I wanted to pop in and see how you were doing."

"Thanks, Mom. I'll talk to you later." Aubrey started to reach out for a hug, but her mother had turned away and walked out the door. *Why is she so reluctant to show me she cares about me? Maybe she doesn't.*

****

When Steve returned to the hospital later in the afternoon, Aubrey was free of her IV and dressed, sitting on the bed.

"Hi, Steve. The doctor says I'm good to go. I have to take it easy, but, of course, I won't."

She laughed at his scowling face.

He laughed with her and said, "Let's get out of here. I think we still have time to pick up Kizzy if you want. Or we can get her tomorrow. Your choice."

"Yes, I'd like to get her. I'm sure she's scared and missing me. Thanks again for taking us in for now."

They left the hospital, Aubrey fussing about having to be taken out in a wheelchair, while Steve pulled his car around. She groaned as she settled in and pulled her seatbelt around her. "Oh, that hurts." She took a few shallow breaths as she waited for the throbbing pain to abate. "Your car smells so much better than that hospital room."

"Thanks. Kizzy will be happy to see you," Steve offered, trying to distract her from her pain.

"I know. Have you heard anything from Brady or Weston about the guy who attacked you? Jim ... Joe ... what's his name?"

"Close. Jeff Phillips. You don't recognize it?"

"No. His name never came up until I was in the warehouse. Larson and Hunter mentioned him. They argued about why he was taking so long killing you. Hunter said you'd probably caught him, and that Jeff was on his way to jail, most likely spilling his guts. Larson thought he was waiting for you to return home from somewhere. I was so afraid for you. Have they found out Larson's first name or where he lives?"

"They're not telling me anything, Aubrey. You may have better luck weaseling information out of them. Let's get you to the house and settled, and I can take you to the station tomorrow morning. Maybe they'll fill us in."

After getting Kizzy from the vet, and trying to restrain the dog's unbridled joy at seeing Aubrey, they headed to Steve's house.

"Poor baby. She looks so pathetic in her little cast." She laughed. "I see everyone at the vet's office signed it for her. I'm furious at Larson for hurting her."

"She'll be okay. We need to catch these guys before they hurt someone else, though. But tonight, you need to relax. You're still healing, and those bruises to your ribs and kidney are going to take time to feel better. You can't work until they are. Besides, you don't want to be on patrol scaring old ladies and little kids with your banged-up face, right?" He grinned at her.

"Ha, ha. Yeah, I looked in the mirror earlier, and it's a mess. That asshole did a number on me, didn't he? But I'm alive, and that's what matters."

They ate pizza and watched M*A*S*H* on TV, enjoying the comfortable companionship they'd developed. Kizzy never left her side. After a while, Aubrey said it was time for bed, and they said goodnight.

****

Kizzy woke everyone early, so she could go outside. Steve didn't have a doggie door like Aubrey had. They enjoyed a leisurely breakfast of juice, toast, eggs, and sausage, then headed to the police station to find answers.

Aubrey took Steve in through the back door to avoid any unnecessary gawking at her multi-colored and bandaged face in the lobby. They made their way to Sergeant Mills's office first.

"Aubrey!" Mills's face lit up but fell when he saw her injuries. "Are you okay to be out of the hospital so soon?"

"Yes, I'm fine. Well, not fine, but I don't need to be sitting in a hospital bed. I'm sure you know Steve Rollins."

"Yeah, hey, Steve." He held his hand out to shake Steve's. "I understand you're the hero who found her. Good job."

"I'm no hero, but I was glad to find her and grateful she wasn't in worse shape."

"You know, I'm right here," Aubrey interjected. "What is happening with Scott Fuller?" Aubrey glared at Mills. "I know Steve told you what he did yesterday."

Mills blew out a breath before answering. He shuffled papers, a never-ending pile always perched precariously on the edge of his desk and finally turned to her. "He's on suspension. He's going to be a problem, I think. He blames all his troubles on you, Aubrey. He'll be out for a week."

He held up his hand before she could object. "I know, but it was out of my control. I thought he should have been fired, but I can't do that without the captain's say-so. He thinks Fuller needs time to sort out whatever, but you watch your back."

"Super. Now I have to watch out for actual serial killers and one of my own colleagues. Any other good news you'd like to share?" Clenching her teeth, she brushed her hand through her hair. *Is this never going to end?*

"Well, yeah, they found Dan Hunter. He didn't even try to get away. I think he thought Larson would take care of you, and he wouldn't have to worry. His father, of course, told him to say nothing. They're waiting on a search warrant. The DA wants to make a deal with him to give up Larson and anyone else involved."

"That's good news, even if he didn't have anything to do with Lori, only Erin Grant. But, he might have been involved in many others that they haven't tied together quite yet, too. They shouldn't give him a deal, not after everything I heard him say," Aubrey said.

"I agree, but I'm not in charge. You need to go upstairs and make a statement in writing."

"Yeah, I know. We're headed there next. By the way, I don't know when the doctor will clear me for work."

"That's fine. Your job right now is to get better. You've been through a lot, and it'll do you good to have some downtime. You did good, Rookie." He winked at her.

She smiled. "Thanks, Sarge. I'll catch you later."

Steve and Aubrey made their way to the Detective's Bureau, hoping to find Weston there alone. They were in luck, and Weston looked up as they entered the room, waving them over to his carefully organized and cleared-of-clutter desk. Family photos and childish drawings signed by his young son decorated his wall.

"Stanton, Rollins. I'm glad you came in." He shook both their hands. "I still need a written statement from you, Officer. We caught Hunter at home. He was packing. I think he was planning a lengthy vacation. Thanks to your information and evidence we found at the warehouse, we may be able to nail him for several murders, as well as Erin Grant's. We're waiting for the warrant to search his house. He's not talking. We didn't expect him to, but the DA's hopeful of cutting a deal with him." He moved some papers on his desk, took out a legal pad, and handed it to her. "Go in the interview room and write out everything you told us while I chat with Steve."

"Sure." She left the two standing with their hands in their pockets.

"So, Steve. Why are you here?" asked Weston.

"I have Aubrey staying with me for the time being. She needs to be protected from the bastard who grabbed her, and she needs someone to take care of her and her dog until they're both healed. Until you get everyone involved in custody, I'm not comfortable with her living alone in her condition right now."

Weston nodded his head. "You're right. I'm glad you can help her out. I think Larson ... his first name's Brent ... ducked out of town. I'm concerned he went to California to see Wyatt. He may have figured out how you knew where to look for her. I've notified the authorities out there to watch for him."

"That's a good idea. I didn't get the impression that Wyatt had anything to do with Lori's murder, but he may have been told about it and didn't reveal what he knew at the time. Maybe they should pick him up?"

"That's a good suggestion. I'll call the Minerva police and ask them to do it." His expression turned serious, eyes narrowed and glaring. "What else do you know that you haven't told me?"

"First, what did Phillips have to say about attacking me?"

"Nothing much. He was told to silence you since you'd been talking to Aubrey. The plan was to kill you to buy them a few days." He finally grinned at his old friend. "I guess you've still got it, old man. I'm glad you took him out instead, or we'd be right back at the starting point. Other than that, he said he didn't know anything more."

"Punk kid. Probably thought he was dealing with some hot-shot criminals. Maybe he thought it would make him a big-shot, too."

"Yeah, maybe. But we got him, Hunter, and soon, we'll have Larson, too. We stopped by his mother's house to see if he was hiding out there. He wasn't. She claimed she didn't know where he was. She seemed pretty shook up when we told her he'd taken Stanton and beaten her. I don't think she had a clue what he was up to all these years."

Weston knocked his knuckles on the desk. "You never know with kids. You do your best, but there's no guarantee how they'll turn out." He shook his head, glanced at a photo of his son and daughter.

"You're right. I wonder how many others he's killed. Any idea?" Steve asked.

"Not yet, but I have a bad feeling there were a lot of 'em. Departments all over the area are combing through their cold case files to see if there are any similarities. It could take years."

Aubrey returned with her statement and looked at the two old detectives. Their expressions and sudden silence as she approached, told her they'd been talking about Larson and his deeds.

"So, when are you gonna catch him?"

"We're working on it. Don't get any ideas in your head, you're off the case now, but I'm proposing a commendation for you," Weston said. "What you did was brave and stupid. You could have been killed because of your inexperience."

Weston hesitated then added, "On the other hand, you helped identify at least three killers, and we're going to do everything we can to keep them off the street. Once you're fully healed, I'll talk to Mills about a detective's shield for you. I think he'll back you on it. It's unusual for a woman to be a detective, especially one as young as you, but I think you'd be a real asset to our department, Aubrey. We'll train you, so you don't get yourself killed, though."

He smiled and hugged her. She winced as the hug squeezed her bruised ribs. "Glad you're going to be okay."

Aubrey stared wide-eyed at Steve. A knowing smile crossed his lips.

Chapter 22

Aubrey and Steve left the station and headed back to his house. She didn't want to leave her dog alone for very long, especially with Larson on the loose. They walked inside and made themselves comfortable on Steve's leather couch and armchair.

"I'm already tired," Aubrey said as she relaxed, Kizzy at her feet. "It's not even noon yet. This is ridiculous."

Steve laughed. "No, it's not. You went through a lot of stress, as well as physical and emotional pain. Your body and mind need time to heal and rest. But we can talk about stuff. What are your thoughts on Larson going to Wyatt? Can you call your brother and see if he's seen him?"

"That's a good idea. I could do that. I'm still not positive Tom isn't involved or knowledgeable about what they were up to, but that's for another day. I could call him now, in fact." She stood and walked to the phone. "It's long distance, do you mind me using your phone for the call?"

"No, go ahead. Call him."

"Hello." Tom's voice sounded distant.

"Hi, Tom, it's me. How ya doin'?"

"Oh, hi, Squirt. I'm good, you?"

"I'm out of the hospital, so I'm happy. Did Mom tell you what happened to me?"

"Yeah, she did. I'm glad you're okay. That must have been pretty scary, being kidnapped and beaten up."

"It was. All I have to do is look in the mirror to remind me." She drew a deep breath. "You know who did it, right? Brent Larson and Dan Hunter."

"Really? No, I didn't know that. I don't even remember Brent, although Greg talked about him. Dan Hunter, huh? That surprises me. I always thought he was a pretty good guy."

"He's definitely not. I was wondering if you'd seen Greg Wyatt in the past couple days?"

"Yeah, I saw him yesterday. Why?"

"Was he with anyone?" she asked, exhaustion heavy in her voice.

"No, but he did call off work. Said he was sick, which is weird, he's never sick and never misses work, now that I think about it."

"For your own good, I'm telling you to stay away from him for the time being. Okay?"

Aubrey glanced at Steve and nodded.

"Well, I don't expect to see him, we're not exactly best friends. Is he a part of this?"

"I can't tell you, but if you do see him, and he's with anyone, let me know right away."

"I can do that." He hesitated. "I'm sorry all this happened to you, Aubrey. Really. I know you were doing your job, and I apologize for being angry with you when we talked the last time."

"It's okay, Tom. Take care of yourself. I'll call you in a few days, and we can catch up."

"Cool. Take care."

Aubrey hung up the phone and turned to Steve. "I think Larson's with Greg. Tom says he never misses work, and he called in sick. He's probably picking up Larson from the airport. Did you tell Weston to have the cops there check out Wyatt's place?"

"I did, but I'm going to call him again with this news. Perhaps the Minerva cops will take it more seriously," Steve said.

Aubrey nervously tapped her fingers on the arm of the couch while she listened to Steve relay the information to Weston. She knew it would be a waiting game now ... waiting for Hunter to spill his guts ... waiting for the California cops to pick up Larson if he's there ...waiting for Jeff Phillips to tell what he knows.

"I hate that I'm not more in the thick of things since I'm the one who found these guys."

Steve chuckled at her impatience. "Trust me, I know how you feel. But you're in no shape to be chasing them. Right now, we need to let the detectives handle it. Maybe once they're all in custody, you can play a role in making sure none of them ever sees the light of day again."

She grimaced at him. "Based on what I overheard, I hope they don't cut a deal with Hunter. He apparently likes to torture people. He better not get off. I want to see him in prison for the rest of his life, along with Larson. Besides, Phillips was willing to kill you to protect Larson. And it seems Wyatt is willing to help him escape. They all need to be in jail."

She stood and paced the room, fidgeting with magazines stacked on the coffee table, picking up and putting down owl figurines on a wall shelf. *Steve's wife must have decorated, and he hasn't changed anything since she died. The wallpaper is out-of-date even if it is in good shape. The whole house is too feminine for him. But, he must like it this way. Probably reminds him of her.* She looked inside a curio cabinet at the Hummel collection that filled every shelf.

"I'm glad Jaime Harris isn't involved, or at least it doesn't appear so. And, of course, I'm glad Tom's not, either."

After a lunch of BLT sandwiches and chips, Aubrey asked, "Steve, could you take me back home, please? I need to get some things, and I'd like to check on the house. Can we take Kizzy, too?"

"Of course, I should've realized you'd need stuff from your place. Let me get my gun, and we can go."

****

Arriving at her house, Aubrey's hands shook. "What am I going to find in there, Steve? Black fingerprint dust? Blood? I want to be prepared."

"Yes, black dust, for sure. Some blood, but not much. Kizzy was outside the back door when I found her, so there's nothing in the house regarding her injuries. I think it'll be okay and I'm here with you every step. Are you all right?"

She took a few deep breaths. *I can do this. I have to.* "Yes, I'm ready." She stepped out of the car and walked toward her front door, which still had the crime scene tape across it. "Is this a problem?" She pointed to the tape.

"No, it shouldn't be. The techs finished two days ago with any evidence inside." He broke the seal and turned the door handle. The door wasn't locked. "Stay back, Aubrey, and let me go in first."

He drew his gun and stepped through the entrance. After a few minutes, he called, "All clear, come on in."

Aubrey, carrying Kizzy, walked into her front hall. It seemed alien to her: furniture askew, black fingerprint dust everywhere, her stuff out of place. The answering machine blinked with a dozen messages. She set down her dog and pushed the button to listen. Two of the calls were her mother.

"Aubrey, are you home from the hospital? Sorry I haven't had time to come up and see you more. Call me when you get this."

Four calls were from Brad; the most recent one, she could hear his concern radiate through the machine. "Bree, are you angry with me? I've called and called, but you never picked up or returned my calls. Have I done something wrong? Please call me back. I'm worried about you."

Steve raised his eyebrows and mouthed *Bree?*

"Yeah, yeah, it's his nickname for me. I didn't even think about telling Brad." *What does that say about our relationship?* "No wonder he's worried. I'm surprised it wasn't in the papers. Do you mind if I give him a call now?"

"No, go ahead. Call your mother, too."

She dialed Brad's number and picked at her cuticles until he answered.

"Hello?"

She smiled and relaxed at his familiar and sexy voice. "Hi, Brad. It's me. I'm so sorry, I should've called you sooner. I got home and listened to the messages. You didn't do anything wrong, but it's a long story. I wanted to let you know I'm fine.

Could we get together, maybe tomorrow? I've got a lot going on right now." *I'm babbling for chrissake.*

"Hi, Bree. I'm glad you called. I was worried about you. I heard on the news about the arrest of a suspect in the murder of Erin Grant and wondered if you were involved. How's your investigation going? Why does your voice sound so different?"

"Well, see, that's what I need to tell you about but not over the phone. Can I call you back tomorrow, and we can set up a time to talk?"

"Sure, of course. I'm glad you're okay. I'll talk to you tomorrow. Thanks for calling."

She hung up and turned to Steve. "I think I'll call my mom back at your house."

They returned to Steve's after she'd gathered her clothes and essentials, including Kizzy's food, doggie treats, toys, blanket, and leash.

Aubrey settled Kizzy's things into a corner in the bedroom she'd be using. Kizzy trailed after her as she walked into the kitchen. Steve was fixing a cup of coffee, pointing to ask if she wanted one. She shook her head.

"Now, I need to call my mother." She looked at the ceiling as her mother answered the phone. "Hi, Mom."

"It's about time you called. I went to the hospital, and they said you were released. Where are you? I drove by your house yesterday, and there's police tape on your door. How embarrassing."

"I know, Mom. It's a crime scene. I was abducted from my house. Remember, it wasn't my fault, it was the guy who took me. He's a killer, so I'm glad I'm alive. I don't care about the tape. I'm staying at Steve's for the time being. We got home late last night, so I didn't want to bother you."

"Fine, but why at his house? If you need help, you could stay here with me. I *am* your mother."

Aubrey turned her head toward Steve. She opened her eyes wide and made a rictus smile, looking aghast. Coffee spurted out his nose as he attempted not to laugh.

"Thanks, Mom, but we're still working on the case, and it's easier if I'm with him. Besides, I'm not sure if the techs have finished collecting evidence at my house yet. And I have Kizzy, who was also injured. I can use his help taking care of her. I'll call you in a day or two." She placed the phone in its receiver.

"That went well." They both laughed.

"Was your mom upset?" he asked.

"Ha, no. She offered to have me stay with her, as I'm sure you figured out, but she doesn't want anyone there, interrupting her busy, single life."

"Well, I'm happy to have you. You could invite Brad to dinner here, so you don't have to go out until you're healed a bit more." He flinched. "I hate to say this, Aubrey, but your face could scare folks, and Brad might need a minute to compose himself when he sees you."

She laughed, then groaned. "Oh, please, don't make me laugh. It hurts. That's a good idea, though. I'll still wait until tomorrow morning to call him back. Maybe my bruises will be a wonderfully mixed green and yellow shade, don't you think? Also, I hope they've caught everyone involved first."

"I agree."

****

Jayne hung up the phone after speaking with Aubrey. Her anger dissipated as she recalled her joy when Aubrey was born. Her friend, Annie, was visiting, waiting to hear what happened on the call Jayne had been so anxious to make.

She turned toward her friend. "I really shouldn't get so mad at her. I know she's doing her job, but I have to protect Tom from her accusations. I can't lose another child." She sat on her sofa and felt the tears form in her eyes. "I've never talked about this, but you're my best friend, and I need to tell someone. A year after Tom was born, I had another baby, a girl. I named her Kristi. She was beautiful and full of life. Tom loved her, too. He treated her like a fragile angel."

"Wow, I'm glad you feel you can tell me, Jayne. What happened to her?" Annie asked, her voice gentle, understanding the answer would be sad.

"When she was a year old, Tom was two and a half at the time, and they were playing in the backyard. I went into the house to get something to drink and left them for a couple of minutes. I realize it must have been longer than I planned because when I came back outside, Annie was floating, facedown, in the pool.

"Tom was crying, and because she was in the deep end, I couldn't rescue her. I never learned how to swim. I was frantic. I screamed and screamed for someone to come help me, but no one heard me. I grabbed the skimmer pole and tried to pull her closer to the edge. When I finally managed to get her close enough, I reached out, almost falling in myself, and pulled her tiny, limp body out of the water. By the time I had her on the deck, she was gone. I called the police, but they weren't able to revive her."

"Oh, my God, Jayne! I'm so sorry. You've never spoken about this before." Annie reached over and held Jayne's hand.

"No, John forbade me to speak of it to anyone. He said it was best forgotten, but I can never forget. How could I? It was a huge problem in our marriage and part of why we divorced. He refused to acknowledge our sweet Kristi ever lived. Then along came Aubrey. She was not as easy a baby as Kristi had been. She didn't have the sunny disposition either." She carefully wiped the corners of her eyes.

"Aubrey didn't sleep, cried all the time. I was always exhausted. She didn't look like Kristi either, which should have made it easier to love her, but it didn't. I wanted Kristi back. I blamed Tom, even though he was only two and certainly couldn't be at fault. It was *my* fault for leaving them, and I've never forgiven myself."

Jayne took a deep breath and continued, "I took it out on Tom, and later, on Aubrey. Neither of them deserved it. I was so afraid of loving them completely, afraid if something happened to one or both of them, I wouldn't be able to bear it. So, I keep them and my emotions at arm's length. I worry every day about Aubrey being a cop, and now she's been hurt. I can hardly look at her, and I constantly think about what I would've done if those horrible men had killed her."

"But she's okay, now. Right?" Annie asked.

"She was severely beaten by one man, but she'll recover. I know it could happen again. I can't stand the fear. What can I do?" She sobbed.

Annie hugged her, telling her, "It'll be all right. Aubrey will be fine. Maybe you should tell her and Tom how you're feeling," she suggested.

Jayne pulled away from her friend. "No! I couldn't, Aubrey doesn't know about Kristi, and I don't think Tom remembers her. He has never spoken about her since that awful day. Please don't tell anyone about this. I couldn't handle it if everyone knew what a horrible mother I am."

"Okay, it's okay, your secret's safe with me."

"I'm so sorry to burden you with this." She wiped her eyes. "Let me fix my makeup and let's go shopping. That always makes me feel better."

"Um, okay, if that's what you want to do," Annie replied. "Maybe we can stop and get something to eat, as well. They have a great new restaurant opposite the mall."

****

The next evening, Brad arrived at Steve's for dinner with a colorful bouquet of mixed flowers for Aubrey. Steve was correct in guessing he would need a moment when he saw her.

As Brad gaped at Aubrey, Steve took the flowers into the kitchen and placed them in a vase. He carried it into the living room, setting it on a shelf.

"Oh, my God, Aubrey. What the hell happened to you?" Brad's eyes widened as he took in the purple and red blotches on her face and gauze bandage on her nose. He went to hug her, but she put her hand out to stop him.

"Sorry, I have bruised ribs." She lifted the corner of her shirt to show him the discoloration on her side and back. "Thanks for the pretty flowers. I love them. The short story is, I was kidnapped by the guy who killed Lori and Erin when he realized I knew who was involved. He held me captive in a warehouse and beat me, a lot. He also broke Kizzy's leg. Steve rescued us. We're staying here while we heal and wait for the detectives to catch him."

Brad stood still, mouth agape. A few seconds went by before he could speak. "I ... I ... don't know what to say. It's stupid to ask if you're okay. Clearly, you're not. Was anything broken other than your nose?"

Aubrey smiled. *He's taking this pretty well.* "Actually, I'm fine. Yes, my nose is broken, and I don't look so good, but I'm lucky. I'm alive. The bruises will go away, my nose will heal. Steve thought it would be easier to stay in and have dinner here, so we don't have the gawping of strangers at a restaurant. Is that all right?"

"Sure. I'm fine with that. By the way, ..." he turned toward Steve, standing on the side of the room, watching. "I'm Brad. Nice to meet you, and thanks for rescuing Aubrey and letting her stay here."

Aubrey smiled. "What's for dinner? I'm starving."

Chapter 23

After a delicious lasagna dinner with salad, garlic bread, and apple pie for dessert, Steve, Brad, and Aubrey chatted in the living room about the Tigers' recent winning streak and the unusually warm weather. Aubrey avoided talking about the investigation or her role in finding the suspected killers.

"I think it's time for this old-timer to go to bed," Steve announced as he stood. "Besides, I'm sure the two of you have plenty to talk about without me hanging around. Good night."

"Night."

Once Steve had closed his bedroom door, Brad turned to Aubrey, fury in his voice. "What were you thinking?"

Surprised and angry at his tone, she looked at him. *Again? He's questioning my ability to do my job? Who the hell does he think he is?* "About what? Trying to catch a killer? That's my job, Brad." She straightened her back and glared. "Besides, Detective Weston said I did such a good job on this, he's putting me in for the Detective's Bureau and thinks my sergeant will back me. As soon as I can return to work, I'm going to. Would you be saying the same thing to a male cop? I don't think so."

"Even after all that's happened, you think you should?" He shook his head. "You're a fairly new officer. Isn't that why you got kidnapped and couldn't defend yourself? I think you need more experience before making such a drastic move."

"Gosh, Brad. Thanks for your support in my career." She scowled at him. "Weston said they'd train me so I can avoid the mistakes I made this time. Do you think I wanted to be knocked out, abducted, and beaten?"

Brad's eyes lowered. "No, of course not. I'm worried about you. Seeing you tonight, in this condition, scared me. He could've killed you if Steve hadn't found you first."

"Trust me, I'm fully aware of the possibilities." She shook her head. "I can see you're concerned about me, but if I'd had more back-up for my investigation like I will as a detective, it probably wouldn't have happened. I would've had a partner who would've known I was missing sooner. He would have also been privy to my discoveries and the people involved. A lot of things would've been different. On the plus side, I found Lori and Erin's murderers, stopped a group of serial killers, gave their families closure, and I would do the same thing again."

Brad blew out a breath. "It makes me nervous. Maybe I'm not the right person to be in your life. I can't handle the danger you're always in." He stood and walked a circle around the room, sat next to her again. "In the short time we've been seeing each other, you've punched someone and broken your knuckles, been kidnapped and beaten, been suspended from work, your dog's been hurt, you've received threatening phone calls, and had a dead possum taped to your door." He looked at her, a question in his eyes.

"Well, when you put it like that, it does sound pretty bad." *He doesn't know about Fuller attacking me, either. I think I'll keep it to myself.* She flipped her hands up and grinned at him, then turned serious. "But it is who I am. I chose this profession to help people. Isn't that why you want to be a lawyer? If you decide to be a defense attorney, won't you be dealing with criminals? If you're a prosecutor, for sure you'll have angry, dangerous people who hate you. How is it any different than what I face every day?" She studied his expression.

"Maybe you're right, Aubrey." He stood again and paced the room. "I haven't had to deal with all that yet, and you're already in the thick of it. How about we take it day by day and see how it goes? I start law school next month, so I'm sure I'll be busier than I am now. It'll give us some time to consider whether we're good for each other or not."

"Honestly? I want someone who supports me, not financially, but emotionally. A partner who champions my goals, and even if he doesn't understand why I want those things, he wants for me what *I* want for me. And I'll do the same for him. If you don't think you can be that guy, perhaps we should say good-bye tonight." Aubrey waited while he appeared to consider the choice. *Have fun in law school, but I doubt I'll be waiting if you come back.*

"I agree with you, Aubrey. I'm not that man, not now. I might become him, but I'm not there yet. I won't ask you to wait for me. I'd like to keep in touch, though, if that's okay."

"Yes, Brad. Maybe law school will open your eyes to the danger we all face every day. We can't avoid it, but we can prepare for it. I wish you well." She pecked his cheek and walked him to the door. "Good night." *Don't bother keeping in touch. You're a nice guy but not the right guy for me.*

As he walked away into the night, Aubrey closed and leaned against the door. Brad was fun, but his repeated complaints about the way she handled situations irritated her. She couldn't envision her life with a man who questioned her every move. She sighed, called Kizzy, and went to bed.

****

The phone's loud jangle woke Steve early the next morning. Steve growled as he answered, "This better be important, it's five o'clock."

Aubrey heard the ringing and muffled sounds from Steve's room. Dressed in a large t-shirt and flannel shorts, she walked across the hallway and stood in his doorway, listening to his side of the conversation.

"When?... Uh-huh ... You're sure? ... Okay. I'll tell her." He hung up the phone.

A huge smile on his face, he said, "The Minerva PD got him. Brent Larson is in custody in California. They caught him at Greg Wyatt's house." He took a breath, pressed his lips together, and delivered the rest of the news. "He killed Greg before the local police could get to him. Apparently, he was trying to dispose of the body when they showed up. Something he said or did, made them think he was going to dump him in the mineshaft."

Aubrey stood wide-eyed, biting her lower lip. "It's over? Truly over?" Her body shuddered and shrugged off her fear like an oversized coat.

"Not entirely, although with the statement Detective Brady got last night from Dan Hunter, it should be a slam dunk. Maybe he'll plead guilty, and we can avoid a trial. I think you can tell the Harris family you found their daughter's killer. It may give them some peace of mind. I can go with you if you want."

"Of course you should go with me. You're the original detective on the case. I know Detectives Weston and Brady will notify Erin's parents. Since it's so early, I'll defer to your experience. What time would you think is appropriate to go over to their house?"

"Don't you want to get more sleep?" He yawned, looking closer at her. "No, I can see you're too excited. I would say around eight. Even if they don't work, they should be up, and the neighbors won't be out in force, rubber-necking, yet. Let's make breakfast and shower, get dressed. I'm concerned about your bruises scaring the daylights out of them." He laughed.

Aubrey playfully punched his shoulder. "Maybe some make-up will hide the worst of it?" She waggled her eyebrows.

****

At eight o'clock, they knocked on the Harris's front door and waited. Aubrey was pleased to see Mrs. Harris open it. She was still in her bathrobe, and Aubrey felt a tinge of embarrassment showing up so early but believed they'd want to know as soon as possible. The smell of fresh coffee wafted through the opening.

"Well, hello, Aubrey, Detective Rollins. News this early is usually bad. Please come in before every neighbor on the block sees you. Honey, your face looks terrible. Haven't you been getting enough sleep?" She squinted at Aubrey's dark circles under her eyes, the gauze bandage on her nose had been removed the previous day.

Aubrey stifled a laugh. "I know, Mrs. Harris. It's a long story with a good ending. Can we sit somewhere?"

A voice from the kitchen interrupted them. "Mary, what's going on? Who's here this early?"

"Ralph, come into the living room. It's Detective Rollins and Aubrey ... er ...Officer Stanton." She smiled at Aubrey and patted her arm, then motioned for everyone to sit. Aubrey sat on the couch before being directed into the too-soft armchair. "Would you two like some coffee? I just made it."

"Detective Rollins, haven't seen you in a long time," Harris offered in a not-so-pleased-to-see-you greeting.

"No, sir. I retired a few years ago. Thanks, Mrs. Harris, but we both had several cups already this morning. Any more, and I know I'll float away. I've been helping Aubrey on your daughter's investigation. I'll let her give you the news." He looked at her and nodded.

"Mr. and Mrs. Harris, I know it's barely eight o'clock, but I thought you'd want to know right away. We have good news for you. We found the man we believe abducted and killed Lori, and he's under arrest. He was in California and is being transported here later today."

Mrs. Harris gasped and covered her mouth.

Mr. Harris stood with his arms crossed and stared at Aubrey. "What the hell happened to you?"

"Lori's alleged killer kidnapped and beat me when I got too close to discovering him. Detective Rollins came to my rescue."

"I thought you said he was in California?" he asked.

"After he realized someone had found me, he fled there to escape capture. But we got him. That's the important part."

"Who was it?" Mrs. Harris asked.

"His name's Brent Larson. His younger brother, Oliver, was friends with Jaime. We don't know if Oliver was involved or not, but he's dead, so I'm not sure it matters. We have no reason to believe Jaime was involved, just so you know. I really can't say more until he's arraigned and whether he pleads guilty or not.

You can tell Jaime and Jake, but please don't share this with anyone else until after his court hearing. I'm sure it will come out in the news."

Mrs. Harris started crying. "We've waited so long to hear this. Thank you both."

Ralph put his arm around his wife to comfort her. "Yes, thank you," he said, as he wiped his eyes.

"We'll see ourselves out. I'm glad we were able to catch him." Rollins stood and nodded toward the door for Aubrey to follow.

Outside the house, she said, "It doesn't bring Lori back, but at least she can now rest in peace."

"Thanks to you." He patted her shoulder.

****

Two days later, knowing Larson had been transported from California and was in custody in the county jail, Aubrey and Kizzy returned home. Happy to be in her own place, she scrubbed the fingerprint dust off everything, mopped floors, reorganized the strewn papers, and relaxed in the comforts of her personal space.

The court arraigned Larson and withheld bail. Dan Hunter, despite his father's erstwhile pleadings, was refused bail, as well. Jeff Phillips's lawyer managed to have him released with a minimal bond, due to the charges being reduced to breaking and entering.

Aubrey's doctor released her for light-duty work to begin the following Monday. She checked on her uniform, making sure it was clean and pressed, shoes shined. She'd been informed of the requirement to see a departmental psychiatrist before being allowed on patrol. She understood the reasons, and it allowed more time for her injuries to completely heal.

She startled when the phone rang. "Hello."

"Aubrey, it's Steve." She heard the urgency in his voice. "Weston called; thought you were still staying here. Larson's escaped. Bring Kizzy and come back, now. Or I can come get you. Make sure your doors are locked, windows, too. Get your gun and keep it handy. He'll either run or go after you. You're the only living witness we know of. If he can silence you, he has a better chance of a reduced charge. Move, now!"

"Got it." She slammed the phone down and ran for her handgun, checked it was loaded, and placed it in a small holster on her waist. She grabbed Kizzy and locked her doors as she left. She glanced around the outside of the house and dashed to her car. Not seeing anything or anyone suspicious, she settled her dog inside and climbed in.

A knock on the driver's side window had Aubrey fumbling for her gun. Her elderly neighbor's face filled the space. Aubrey blinked her eyes furiously trying to contain her fright. Her heart pounding, she rolled down the window.

Her voice quivered as she asked, "Mrs. Andrews, can I help you?" She tried to look around the woman, but the woman's head blocked her view.

"Oh, no, dear. I saw you run out of your house like the devil was chasing you, and thought I'd check —"

The woman's head exploded with a thud, spraying Aubrey with blood, bone, and brains.

She scrambled for her weapon, still not seeing the assailant's position. Wiping the gore from her face with her left arm, she turned the key in the ignition and squealed out of her driveway. *Forget the gun. I need to get out of here.* Gunshots hit the side of the car, and Aubrey ducked down as far as she could and raced away.

She considered going to Steve's house. *No, I'll lead them right to him. I need to go to the station. I can get help there.* She took a shuddering breath. *I can't let Larson take me again.* Her hands shook on the steering wheel. Aubrey bit down on her lip to keep the tears at bay. *I need to stay focused.* She sped through town toward safety. Sliding the car sideways into the employee parking lot, she threw open her door, grabbed the dog, and ran inside.

She shouted for Sergeant Mills; found him looking bewildered in the break room.

"Sarge, Larson's escaped and just tried to kill me." Her fear tumbled out of her mouth. "He shot one of my neighbors and might be heading to Steve's house. Or he might be coming here. We need to be prepared for either. I need to call Steve and tell him."

"Okay, Stanton. Calm down. Tell me exactly what happened." His eyebrows furrowed as he took in the blood and brain matter on her face and clothes.

"There's no time. He could be at Steve's right now. I have to call him now. We also have to be ready if he shows up here." She grabbed the nearest phone and started dialing.

"Rollins."

"Steve, get out of there. He came after me, shot my neighbor. I'm at the station. He—"

The sound of gunshots and shouting filled the handset. She turned to Mills, "He's at Steve's house. Send someone to help him!"

The phone went dead.

Chapter 24

Aubrey paced the floor of the squad room. Sergeant Mills took her and Kizzy to his office and shut the door, grabbing Aubrey's arms, avoiding the blood on her sleeves, to stop her frantic motion.

"Larson escaped earlier, but he was caught almost immediately. Look at me." His eyes bore into hers. "Whoever shot at you, it wasn't him. Patrol cars are on their way to Rollins's house. I have no idea who's there, but we should hear something soon. Try to calm down."

"Calm down? Calm down? How can I calm down when I know someone is trying to kill Steve?"

In a quiet voice, holding her gaze, he said, "Aubrey, Steve can take care of himself. Trust him. You know—"

An officer knocked, then entered the office and whispered to Mills.

An exasperated sigh escaped the sergeant's lips as he turned to Aubrey. "They have the shooter in custody. Rollins is fine." He paused. "It was Scott Fuller. Apparently, he was looking for you there, after he lost you at your house."

"What? Why?" She blinked at him in confusion. "At the hospital, he did say he'd do anything to have me removed. I didn't think he meant he'd kill me." She shook her head.

"They're bringing him in now. Stay here. I don't want a confrontation between you two."

"I'm angry, but I'm fine." She hissed.

He looked her in the eye and said, "It's not a suggestion. Stay here."

Aubrey glared at him but closed the door after he left. She sat on the floor and cuddled Kizzy. "It's okay, baby," she said more to herself than the dog.

The arresting officers marched Fuller through the phalanx of cops and secured him in a holding cell. Aubrey heard Mills talking to a couple of them. "Did he give you any trouble?"

"Nah, he gave up when we arrived. It didn't hurt that Rollins had punched him, and he was lying on the ground, with

Rollins's foot on his neck, and a .357 pointed at his head." They laughed. "The old guy's still got it."

Aubrey heaved a sigh of relief. *Thank you again, Steve. How many times have I said that?* She walked out of the office, approached Mills and the other officers. One was Mark Jacobs, the cop she'd gone to the bar and had a drink with, once.

"Hey, Mark. Thanks for bringing him in. Did you guys order the crime scene techs to both mine and Steve's house?"

"Yeah, that was ordered before we got him in the car. I never would have expected something like this from him. I guess you did, though. You said as much when we were at the bar that night." His sheepish grin showed his embarrassment. "By the way, I'm glad you're all right. You know … after your … ordeal. You know you have brains and blood all over you, right?" He raised his eyebrows.

"Yes, I do, and I know I stink. Thanks. I'll be fine, and now with everyone in jail, that should help." She smiled at him. "How's Steve?"

"He's okay. He knew something was up and had his gun with him when Fuller showed up. He admitted he was caught off guard when he saw who it was. Your neighbor is dead. I guess you knew that already. I'm sorry."

"Thanks. I'll bet he was. I feel bad for Mrs. Andrews. Did they cover her up?"

"We didn't go to your house, but I'm sure they took care of her."

Steve walked in and gingerly hugged Aubrey. "I'm glad you're okay, but you're covered in bad stuff. You need to get cleaned up." He turned toward Mills. "She needs to go home, shower, and change. You've got your man, there's no reason to keep her here."

The sergeant nodded. "I know, but she needs to give a statement first." To Aubrey, "Go to the interview room and write out what happened, starting with the incident in the hospital with Fuller. Go clean up ... and don't forget your dog. Take him with you while you do your report. I need my office."

"Right away, Sarge."

"I'm going to wait for Aubrey. Do you want my statement, too?" Steve asked.

"Of course. Use the other room."

After Aubrey and Steve had completed their statements and answered questions, they walked out together to the parking lot.

"It's been quite a day, hasn't it? Are you comfortable going home?" Steve asked.

She drew in a breath. "I hope they've taken care of Mrs. Andrews. She was a kind old lady and only wanted to check on me. She died as a result of her concern. What do I tell her family?"

"You tell them she was worried about you and saved your life. If she hadn't been standing in front of your car window, you might have taken that bullet. You don't have to tell them that part."

Aubrey blinked away tears. "So many deaths, it's so heartbreaking." She swiped her eyes, coughed, and spoke again. "I hope they all rot in jail. Larson will be brought up on murder charges in California, too, won't he?"

"Yeah, he should be. If they connect him to more murders here, other than Lori and Erin, though, he may get so many life sentences, they'll never get their shot at him. We can only hope."

"Thanks again, Steve. I need to get home with Kizzy. I'll call you later tonight after I've settled in." She hugged him and left.

****

Aubrey arrived at Donna's the next day for their Memorial Day barbeque, without her promised guest.

"Where's your mystery man?" Donna hugged her friend. Scowling at Aubrey's appearance, she asked, "And what happened to your face, girl?"

Aubrey returned the hug and wrinkled her nose. "It's a long story. I'll tell you later. As for the mystery man, his name is Brad, and I broke up with him the other night."

"That didn't take long. Had you gone out with him much?"

"A while. He seemed to find fault with how I did my job. That doesn't work for me, so I told him to take a hike. It was a shame, too. When he wasn't giving me a hard time, I liked him."

"Ahh, I'm sorry, Aubrey. You don't want someone like that anyway. You'll find the right guy soon, I'm sure."

"Well, well, well. Look who the cat dragged in." Donna's husband, Pete, walked over and hugged Aubrey, who winced at the tight hold around her bruised and sore ribs.

Pete, at twenty-five, already sported a receding hairline. Not that it bothered him, his vivacious personality and self-deprecating humor endeared him to everyone. He readily hugged anyone he knew and sometimes, people he didn't. Donna's affable temperament, quick wit, and easy laugh made them a perfect couple. Aubrey envied the close family they'd made. Even though Donna complained about their children being wild animals, Aubrey knew how much she doted on their every wish, and disciplined with kindness and patience.

"Hi, Pete. Good to see you, too." She saw him studying her multi-colored bruises on her face. "I know, 'What happened to my face?' I'll tell you both later. Who else is here?"

"Besides the kids, mostly people you know. Come on, I'll introduce you to the ones you don't." Donna hooked her arm through Aubrey's as the two old friends walked toward a crowd of people laughing.

Aubrey spent the afternoon visiting, eating traditional BBQ fare of hamburgers, hotdogs, and potato salad, playing yard games, and relaxing to the soft rock music playing from the outdoor speakers. *Finally, I can unwind. I should spend more time doing things like this.* After a rousing water balloon fight, she said her goodbyes, leaving before the fireworks started.

At home, Kizzy barked, waiting to go outside to do her business. Aubrey let the dog out the back door. After the dog had been hurt by Larson, she still locked Kizzy's doggy door when she wasn't home. The light blinking on her answering machine caught her eye as Aubrey walked through the kitchen. She pressed the button, smiling when she heard Jake's voice.

"Hey, Aubrey. I skipped Kenya when my mom called and told me you'd found my sister's killer. I'm in town for a while. Would you like to have dinner tomorrow night?"

Maybe everything will be all right, after all.

Acknowledgments

I cannot express enough appreciation to the many people who made this book possible.

The completion of this novel could not have been accomplished without the support of my excellent, brutal, but caring, writing groups: the Avon Park Wordsmiths, the Lake Placid Ridge Writers, the many kind and generous people on Scribophile, my daughter and voracious reader like myself, Kyla, who suffered through a few versions and continued to be supportive and helpful, and championed my work, my daughter, Sara, who encouraged my desire to be an author, and my Beta readers: particularly my granddaughter, Sarah, and friends, Kristin and Allyson, who all lead busy lives but were willing to take on the challenge.

My heartfelt thanks.

Avery Stark   November 2019

Keep reading for a sample of Aubrey Stanton's next adventure in:

Solace: Book Two - an Aubrey Stanton novel by Avery Stark

Prologue

I was born half a person. I know, people say that can't happen. A person is either a full person or not, they can't be half. But trust me, I was, and still am. What actually makes a person whole? Is it personality, or simply the body? Is someone who is missing an arm or a leg a whole person? Of course, they are. So, what makes half a person? Mental illness where they can't reason, or imagine, or do their inner thoughts terrorize them? Do bad thoughts make them less whole?

I remember a movie from years ago where a woman, an opera singer, had a benign brain tumor and needed surgery. Her surgeon was Spock. Yes, Leonard Nimoy, of all the actors they could have chosen. Maybe that's why I remember it so vividly.

He cut open her scalp, removed a portion of her skull, and started work. The brain was angry and swelled, too fast, and so much, Spock, frustrated and irritated at the result of his attempts, chose to cut off the swollen part, randomly, viciously. He put her skull back on, sutured her scalp in place. He told his fellow doctors she wouldn't live long and left the OR.

Speaking of ORs, it's funny how many abbreviations the medical community uses: OR, ER, EMT, MI, TIA, and the list goes on into infinity. Is it because they think it's too hard to say the full words, or because their time is so hurried, they can't waste a single second on speaking whole words if an abbreviation will convey the message?

Anyway, the woman in the story, a true story, apparently, not only lived but recovered, only to need another brain surgery years later, choosing Spock once more. I'm not sure I would have preferred him again, and I don't recall the outcome of the second time around, nor do I care.

Hemispherectomies are an interesting surgery. I was surprised at how often they are performed. Over half a million a year worldwide. Amazing, isn't it? Doctors remove half the brain to control severe seizures or brain cancers, usually in children. They claim the brain, whichever side is left, takes on the functions of the one that is missing. I have to believe they're correct, or wouldn't they have stopped doing them? It takes time, of course, for the person to relearn things, like after a stroke. But, after a stroke, many times, things don't come back. Walking, speaking, impulse control, or vision are sometimes lost forever. It makes no sense that a child can lose half his or her brain and be perfectly normal, and whole, but an adult can't.

Time. Things take time. Everyone says so, so it must be right, right? Time, though, is imaginary. Time bends and weaves, changes as a person circles the earth. While sleeping, the clock dictates how much time is passing. Tossing and turning, dreamless and sleepless, watching the minutes tick by. Is the body aging, every minute? Are we wasting time while we attempt to sleep, or is there no way to actually waste time? It's there, whether we sleep or not. We see the progression of time on our bodies, how they sag, and wrinkle, grow flaccid, and spotted.

Yet, when we look back on our lives, can we not see ourselves in our youth? Remember our first date, our first car, our first pet? We recall vivid memories from decades ago, but don't remember why we walked into a room this morning. Does time make us more, or less, whole?

So, back to my original thought. I was born half a person. How is this possible? I am a twin. My very first cells split apart, taking half of me into another person's eventual body. My sister is half a person also. We each have half a brain, mine is the right side, hers the left. The doctors say we are a medical miracle, that some organs simply don't split in half at the stage when they believe ours did. The CT scan shows differently. One kidney each, one lung, half a brain, one ear, one eye, one ovary. We are not conjoined twins, in case anyone is wondering.

We are each twenty years old. We have precisely the same hue of cobalt blue eye and vanilla blonde hair. We have opposite likes and dislikes. She loves baby animals and charity work. I love murder.

Made in the USA
Las Vegas, NV
02 January 2021